CHRISTMAS REDEMPTION

A JON SMITH SHORT STORY

BOB ASHER

BOB ASHER

First Edition 2024

ISBN-13: 978-1-958115-06-0
ISBN-13: 978-1-958115-07-7

This is a story of fiction. The names, characters, organizations, places, events, and incidents are either products of my imagination or are used fictitiously.

Books by Bob Asher
Jon Smith Military/Espionage Thrillers
BEAR TRAP
SMOKE SIGNALS (a Jon Smith Short Story)
ESCAPE FROM DONETSK
FLASH OVERRIDE (Coming soon)

Zack Goodson Crime Thrillers
HOPE IS DEAD

Please join my newsletter using the link below for updates on future Jon Smith novels and short stories and I will give you a FREE copy of my Jon Smith Short Story, SMOKE SIGNALS. I promise I won't sell or share your email address with others.
Bob Asher Books Newsletter
Dedication
Book Cover Design and Interior Formatting by 100Covers.

Once again, thank you, Sierra Kilo, for your patience and unwavering support while I locked myself up in my office at night to write this story.

CHAPTER 1

0715, DECEMBER 24, DAY 1, FLORENCE MEDICAL CENTER, FLORENCE, COLORADO.

"Listen up, Dr. Devilin. You're here for a routine procedure, so if you make trouble at any point, we'll put you back in the van and return to the facility. Give respect and you'll get respect. Do you feel me?" the Bureau of Prisons or BOP guard, Terrance Washington asked. Washington led the detail of eight guards: four in the armored prison van with Devilin, two in a Ford Explorer leading the convoy, and two more in a Ford Explorer following the van. Dr. Luc Devilin merited this high level of security because he was a bona fide, card-caring mad scientist who had murdered hundreds of people by torture during his cruel experiments.

Before his arrest and conviction, Colonel Devilin had been the commander of the US Army Medical Research Institute of Infectious Diseases or USAMRIID located at Fort Detrick, Maryland.

Its mission was to provide leading-edge medical capabilities to deter and defend against current and emerging biological threat agents. He conducted unsanctioned gain-of-function experiments on unwilling subjects in a remote cabin in West Virginia. Gain-of-function was a polite way of saying he was trying to make diseases more infectious and lethal to humans.

According to him, the deaths were necessary in his quest to find cures for the deadliest diseases suffered by mankind. By all accounts, he had a radical personality change shortly before he began his reign of terror. Friends and colleagues all gave similar testimony at his trial. It was as if he had become a different person. Some thought he was possessed.

Devilin smiled and nodded from the bench seat he was chained to across from Washington before saying, "Yes, I understand, Officer Washington." He was an average-sized man with a gigantic intellect and an ego to match it. He was always the smartest man in the room, and he knew it.

The convoy stopped in front of the lower-level parking garage entrance reserved for hospital employees. "How does it look out there?" Washington asked over his portable radio. The four guards in the Explorers had dismounted and taken up their positions; two covering the van and the other two checking inside the entrance. Two hospital security officers held the doors open and a third held the elevator for them, so they didn't have to wait while being exposed.

"It's all clear. The security guards have the elevator standing by for us," BOP Officer Edgar replied.

"Okay, we're coming out," Washington said. Seconds later, the rear door opened and Devilin stepped down to the pavement wearing ankle and belly chains, escorted by Washington and the other guard. Devilin shuffled through the entrance and continued toward the elevator.

As the group passed by, Officer Edgar noticed something unusual about the security guards and said, "Hey, when did you guys start carrying pistols?"

The guard next to him replied, "Today," as he drew his Glock and started shooting. Edgar went down immediately, mortally wounded.

"Get down!" Washington shouted to Devilin as he pushed him to the floor while drawing his pistol and firing. He felt a round crash into the rear ceramic plate in his body armor, taking his breath away and buckling his knees.

The other BOP officers joined in, turning on Edgar's assailant and riddling him with bullets from their Glocks.

Two more security guards appeared from inside the elevator and joined their cohorts shooting the BOP guards in their backs before rushing forward to finish them with shots to the back of their heads. The fight was over in four seconds.

One of the guards from the elevator bent over Washington to finish him. "Wait!" Devilin shouted, "Give me his pistol." The security guard did as ordered. "Officer Washington, do you hear me?" Devilin asked loudly and then kicked him to get his attention. Washington moaned and opened his eyes with great difficulty. Devilin smiled and said, "Do you feel me?" before shooting Washington in the face. Devilin laughed as he handed the Glock off to the security guard.

"Come with me Doctor," he said. The guards and Devilin walked quickly out of the hospital and climbed into a white Ford Sprinter van. The driver calmly drove out of the parking garage and disappeared into the flow of traffic.

"Have you followed my orders?" Devilin asked the mercenary team leader, Salazar.

"Yes, Patrón. To the letter. We are on schedule," he replied. Five minutes later the van pulled into a rented garage. Salazar quickly removed Devilin's restraints, and they all changed clothes and donned heavy winter coats. Another ten minutes later, the overhead garage door opened, and they drove away in a red Honda Pilot and gray Chevrolet Tahoe. A block later, the Pilot rolled through a stop sign. They had traveled two blocks when a black Florence PD Dodge Charger appeared in the Pilot's rearview mirror with its blue and red lights flashing. The police officer depressed his air horn button twice instead of activating his siren. Salazar immediately motioned to his driver to pull to the curb and keyed the microphone on his encrypted radio, "Take him out before he can call us in."

"Roger," came the response as the Tahoe stopped next to the police cruiser and an arm extended out of the passenger window with a suppressed Glock 17.

"Excuse me, officer," the Tahoe's passenger shouted from his open window. The officer turned his head to respond and was shocked to see the fiery flash that killed him. The Pilot and Tahoe pulled away without anyone noticing anything amiss. Ten minutes later, Devilin and his gang boarded a tour bus with forty-five excited tourists headed to Glacier National Park in Montana next to the Canadian border. The sixteen-hour drive to the park included an hour-long break for food, fuel, and a fresh driver.

CHAPTER 2

2330, DECEMBER 24, DAY 1, LAKE MCDONALD HOTEL, GLACIER NATIONAL PARK, MONTANA

Montana State Trooper Jed Patterson stood next to his Gray Ford Explorer Police Interceptor drinking coffee. The blizzard was increasing in strength and the temperature was dropping. The hotel staff had plowed the brightly lit asphalt parking lot an hour earlier in anticipation of the tourists who would be arriving soon. There were already three inches of heavy new snow surrounding Trooper Patterson's cruiser. He was off duty now but decided to hang around because National Park Service Park Ranger Stacy Terrell was still working. She had agreed to extend her shift to cover for a ranger who called in sick. Now her shift would end at midnight. He was freezing his tail off but didn't want to be hiding from the weather inside his nice warm vehicle when Stacy came outside.

Ranger Terrell was one of the few Law Enforcement Rangers assigned to the park. She exited the hotel's front entrance and approached Trooper Patterson. "Thanks for keeping me company, Jed. I can leave as soon as the last bus full of tourists arrives and checks into the hotel. We can't have any of them stumbling around out here all night and freezing to death," Stacy said.

"No problem. Here I brought you some coffee from Kalispell," Jed replied.

"Oh good! Thank you!" she said before accepting the cup and taking a sip.

"So how many people are coming in tonight?" Jed asked.

Stacy pulled her phone from her pocket to check the time. It was 11:32 PM. "The last bus should be arriving any minute. It has fifty-three passengers," Stacy replied. Seconds later, headlights appeared in the distance shining above the snow-covered trees. Soon they could hear the bus's diesel engine laboring up the slope. "Here it comes. Right on time," Stacy said. The bus lumbered into view and turned into the mostly plowed parking lot. Within a couple of minutes, the bus driver had the luggage compartments open, and passengers started exiting the bus to pick up their bags. The crowd was mostly subdued due to the long bus ride. Many had been napping until minutes ago. Stacy and Jed watched from forty feet away as they leaned against the front fender of Jed's cruiser.

The last ten tourists to leave the bus followed the others to the luggage compartments but they seemed different from the others. They were all men, tall, and obviously physically fit even though covered in heavy coats and gloves. They were fully alert and moved as a unit as if every member was responsible for scanning a specific sector of their surroundings. The last man off the bus was smaller and more unsure of himself.

Jed studied the last man as he waited with the others. He seemed familiar. Jed set his cup down on the hood of his cruiser to free his gun hand as he continued to scan the men. "Stacy put down your coffee and get behind the cruiser," Jed said to her as he continued to study the men.

"What is it, Jed?" Stacy asked as she set her cup down next to Jed's.

"I'm not sure. Something's not right. The group of men that got off the bus last are switched on like they are ready to fight. Jed pulled his phone from his pocket and scrolled through several pages until he found what he was looking for. "Look at this," he said as he showed Stacy his phone.

She looked at the phone and then the little man next to the bus. "Oh my God! It's him!" she whispered.

"Just stay cool," Jed said softly as he put his phone away. He keyed the microphone clipped to his jacket to report the sighting and request backup.

***

"Patrón, the policeman has seen you. He is calling for help," Salazar reported.

"Desperate times call for desperate measures. Kill the men and use the women and children for shields. Don't harm the park ranger. She can guide us to the border," Devilin ordered.

"Sí, Patrón," Salazar replied. He pulled a HK MP5 from his bag as he shouted to his men in Spanish, "Mata a los hombres y utiliza a las mujeres y a los niños como escudos humanos. Salva al guardaparque. Ella puede guiarnos a la frontera." Five men and women who were Spanish speakers screamed and immediately ran toward the trooper and hotel. Salazar switched his safety lever from safe to burst and mowed them down. The crowd panicked as the other mercs shot the remaining men and grabbed women and children.

***

Jed threw his arm around Stacy's shoulders and hurried her around the Explorer to take cover. At first, he thought he couldn't return fire for fear of hitting one of the hostages. "Shoot over their heads to keep them away from us!" he shouted to Stacy. She drew her 9mm SIG Sauer P320 pistol and began firing. "King Radio, King 42! Shots fired at police at Lake McDonald Hotel! Escapee Luc Devilin and his men are killing tourists! Mass casualties! Send SWAT ASAP!" Jed transmitted before opening his passenger door to retrieve his Rock River Arms M4 rifle. It was loaded with a thirty-round magazine. Its vertical foregrip housed a light and green laser.

"Stacy, keep firing from the rear bumper. I'll shoot from the front!" Jed shouted before duck-walking to the front passenger tire. He popped up over the hood, placed his green laser on the nose of a mercenary holding a little girl up in front of himself, and fired a 5.56mm 62-grain full metal jacketed bullet into the man's face from fifty feet away in less than two seconds. The man collapsed in a heap as if his internal circuit breaker had been tripped and the girl ran to her mother who was being held hostage by another merc.

Jed dropped down behind the tire as Devilin's gang concentrated their anger on him. A torrent of rounds was absorbed by the cruiser's sheet metal skin and six-cylinder engine block before a single round skipped off the asphalt pavement under the cruiser, tumbled through one of the holes in the aluminum wheel, and shattered Jed's unprotected kneecap. Jed yelped in pain before falling onto his back with his head toward the front bumper, his rifle grip still in his right hand. He looked under the cruiser's radiator and saw a lone, arrogant merc casually walking toward him, no human shield, and his submachine gun held by only one hand leaving it pointed at the ground. Jed rotated his rifle 90° to rest its magazine on the pavement and flipped the selector switch from fire to burst. He lined up his front sight and rear ghost ring peephole on the shitbum's chest and sent him a three-round burst. He was satisfied to see the smug asshole drop face-first into the three inches of snow covering the parking lot before the other mercs sent him a devastating fusillade to silence him.

Stacy fired the last round from her third magazine before turning to Jed to ask for more ammo. She saw him lying motionless with a pool of blood growing in the snow around his head and chest She shouted, "Jed!" She felt sick to her stomach as she fell to her knees.

"Young lady lay down your weapon and join us! It's alright! We are only killing men tonight!" Devilin shouted. Men appeared at both ends of the cruiser pointing rifles at her. She placed her empty pistol on the snow and stood up. "Very good!" Devilin said before turning his attention to Salazar. "Let's borrow the hotel's shuttle bus and start heading north before this blizzard blocks our avenue of escape."

"Sí, Patrón. What of the women and children?" Salazar asked.

Devilin looked around the snowy parking lot at the dead men scattered before him and their wailing wives and children. "They are of no further use to me," Devilin replied matter of fact.

"And the people inside the hotel?" Salazar asked.

"Well, we don't have all night. Let's not be greedy," Devilin said as he smiled.

Salazar turned and shouted orders to his men. They turned and without any outward display of emotion systematically began executing the families.

CHAPTER 3

"Hey, Boss, how much longer until we give Angie a callsign?" Jon transmitted over the team radio as he smiled at Angie. The six-man team was sitting in the cabin of an Agency MH-60 DAP Black Hawk helicopter bathed in red light to preserve their night vision.

Angie was sitting across from Jon. He silently mouthed 'asshole' to Jon.

"Well, I don't know, Streetwalker. He hasn't done anything stupid enough to get a good callsign yet. Unlike the rest of you knuckleheads. Isn't that right, Roadkill?" Boss asked as he turned to look at his second in command, Charlie 2. He got stuck with Roadkill after he picked up a dead armadillo on the side of the road during survival training in the Florida swamps of Hurlburt

Field on Eglin AFB. He and his team hadn't had anything to eat in three days, so he cooked it up and they ate it. It tasted like chicken.

"How'd I get sucked into this? I was just sitting here minding my own business," Roadkill complained. Charlie 3 chuckled. "What are you laughing at? Why don't you tell Angie and Jon how you got your callsign!" Charlie 3's eyes went wide, and he shook his head adamantly. "'No? Okay, I'll tell them. You see, our young Navy SEAL on his first deployment was on liberty in Thailand sharing a hot fudge sundae loaded with whipped cream with his date when his swim buddy walked over and whispered in his ear, 'Hey, man! This bar girl's a dude.' His eyes bugged out so big,'" Roadkill turned to look at Spooge and said as he pointed, "Yeah! Just like that and he choked so bad he spewed whipped cream out of his nose and mouth all over her face!'" Now everyone including the air crew was laughing.

"Okay, listen up, ladies," Boss transmitted over the team radio to his SOG team as they flew along at 10,000' MSL, "Tonight's mission remains the same as the last three. We'll be seizing another missile alert facility tonight. This one is MAF A-01 on Malmstrom Air Force Base, grid coordinates, 47.2817, -110.8008. The 341st Missile Wing's CO knows we are coming but his 10th Missile Squadron and 341st Security Forces Group don't. Once we hit the ground, they will be notified that it's just an exercise. Leave your packs and live ammo on the chopper. We'll jump from 10,000' MSL so we don't need oxygen. Elevation at the MAF is approximately 4000 feet, so pull at 7000 feet. The rest of the brief is the same. We'll be over the drop zone in five minutes. Check your buddy's parachute and standby."

"Charlie 1, we just received a mission abort call. Do you copy?" Ghost 11, the pilot in command, called from the cockpit over the team's radio.

"Roger, I copy. What's going on?" Charlie 1, AKA, Boss asked as he showed the team a thumbs-down signal.

"You'll receive a FRAGO in a minute. You are being retasked for a real-world mission at Glacier National Park. We were told to buster to Malmstrom to pick up extreme cold weather and mountain gear for you," Ghost 11 replied.

The team immediately began swapping out their blanks for live rounds. Jon and Angie grinned at each other and shared a fist bump. They had quietly complained to each other about how boring these training missions had become. The team's chest-mounted ATAK-equipped tablets lit up with an incoming message from SAC/SOG HQ in Langley. Everyone opened their tablets and began reading.

> Charlie Team, proceed to Glacier National Park via Malmstrom AFB ASAP to capture or kill escaped Federal Inmate Dr. Luc Devilin and the mercenary team that is aiding him. He was confined on death row awaiting execution. During a trip to a local hospital, his mercenaries ambushed and gunned down eight BOP guards in cold blood. Devilin is a National Security threat to the citizens of the United States. He is an expert in the modification and disbursal of communicable diseases. During his sentencing, he vowed to eradicate the American population at his first opportunity.

A Montana State Trooper spotted Devilin exiting a bus full of tourists at the Lake McDonald Hotel in Glacier National Park at approximately 2335 hr. Devilin's mercenaries engaged the trooper and an NPS Park Ranger named Stacy Terrell. The trooper killed two of the mercs before he was overwhelmed. They took Ranger Terrell hostage before they summarily executed 41 civilians at the park to celebrate Christmas. Intel indicated they were attempting to pass through the park and cross the Canadian border. If you are unable to engage Devilin before he enters Canada, you are ordered to pursue him until he is in custody or dead.

You can expect 2.5 to three feet of snow on the ground currently and it is expected to snow for the next four days. Temperatures will be between 0°F and 15°F.

Read the following oath aloud:

"I, do solemnly swear that I will support and defend the Constitution of the United States against all enemies, foreign and domestic; that I will bear true faith and allegiance to the same; that I take this obligation freely, without any mental reservation or purpose of evasion; and that I will well and faithfully discharge the duties of the office on which I am about to enter. So help me God."

You are hereby transferred to the United States Marshals Service as Special Deputy United States Marshals for the duration of this mission.

"Okay, marshals read as much of the background information HQ provided as you can," Boss transmitted.

***

"Five miles from Malmstrom," the copilot, Willi called out over the ICS.

"Roger, landing checks," the pilot, callsign Deacon replied.

"Tail wheel switch locked, parking brake off, crew, passengers, and mission equipment check," Willi replied.

"All set in back," the door gunners confirmed.

"Landing checks complete," Willi announced over the ICS before switching to Malmstrom AFB Common Traffic Advisory Frequency or CTAF, 271.9 MHz and transmitted, "Malmstrom Radio, Army Helicopter 98086, five miles southeast for landing on Helipad #2." They were actually flying in an Agency helicopter, but people asked fewer questions when they posed as an Army chopper. Malmstrom had deactivated their runway long ago, so they didn't need an air traffic control tower, but they still hosted Air Force UH-1N Huey and MH-139 Grey Wolf helicopters there to provide support to the Minuteman ICBM missile launch facilities scattered across northcentral Montana. The CTAF allowed pilots flying into or near Malmstrom to make themselves known to each other. The base was brightly lit, but Helipad #2 wasn't so Deacon landed using his NVGs.

A white Ford box van was already loitering nearby. As soon as the helo touched down, the van parked alongside just outside of the rotor arc. Two airmen opened the back doors and began wrestling with the overstuffed OD green parachute bags full of cold weather and mountain gear. Boss transmitted over the team radio to Deacon, "We'll hop out and help them." Deacon replied with two clicks. "Spooge, Reaper. Go help them," Boss transmitted. Spooge shot Boss a why me look expressing his disappointment. "Don't even start bitching. You're young and strong, and you're sitting next to the door. And close the door when you leave. We don't want all this warm air to escape." The other four laughed as they stomped off toward the van.

CHAPTER 4

"Charlie 1, this is Ghost 11. We're five minutes from the southern edge of the park. Do you want us to land at the coordinates on Agassiz Glacier provided by Langley?" the pilot asked.

"Negative. Fly over it at 12,000' MSL and we'll free fall in," Boss replied. "Okay, boys you know what to do. Stay close to me. I'm going first. I'll pop at 3,000' AGL so open your chutes above mine. Give your battle buddy's chute and equipment a good look. We don't want to lose any of our gear," Boss said before checking Roadkill's gear. The team had spent the last couple of hours inventorying their gear and strapping things like snowshoes to the outside of their packs. Over their extreme cold weather clothing, they wore white Arctic camouflaged smocks and trousers to match their white insulated Arctic Mickey Mouse or Bunny boots.

***

"Don't get me wrong, Angie. I'm rarin' to go, but it's going to be cold as Hell out there," Jon said.

"It can't be worse than your Alaska mission, eh, mate?" Angie asked.

"What Alaska mission," Jon replied as he lowered his four tubed GPNVGs over his clear Wiley eye pro. Over two and a half years later, the Eek Lake, Alaska rescue mission was the worst kept secret in the Intel Community. Jon and his ad hoc team of red shirts had defeated a much larger force of Russians, captured two submarines, and killed a double agent before he could escape. He received the Navy Cross for his actions. The citation was classified as TS/SCI.

"Two minutes," the pilot transmitted over the secure team radio's frequency.

"Roger that. Open the doors and get in position," Boss called. Both cabin doors slid back in the locked position and one at a time three men sat on the deck on each side and slid their legs out of the helo to dangle in the slipstream. Boss was sitting on the left side closest to the tail. Roadkill and Spooge sat to his right. Jon would be the first to jump on the right side followed by Angie and their sniper, Charlie 6, callsign Reaper.

"Thirty seconds," the pilot announced. Everyone waited anxiously. Then finally he said, "Go."

Boss leaned forward and fell out of the helo with arms and legs spread wide. In less than five seconds the rest of the team was stacked up above and behind him silently following his path through the heavy swirling snow. Everything was copacetic until they descended through 3000' AGL or above ground level and began opening their ram-air parachutes. A string of bright green tracer rounds rose up at them from the snowy slope. "Dammit! Everybody spread out and start evasive maneuvers! They must have goggles!" Boss transmitted excitedly. Instantly, six parachutes began zigzagging across the sky like a flying circus.

"At least we know we're in the right spot," Jon said sarcastically as the team turned behind Boss and continued their unorthodox descents.

"Follow me. Let's try to land about a mile behind them and below the crest of the hill," Boss called out as he turned his parachute away to the right, "Is anybody hit?"

Reaper being the last man could see his five teammates in front of and below him. "Boss, Reaper, everyone looks good," he transmitted.

Boss glided above the snow bleeding off his airspeed. At fifty feet he released his rucksack to dangle on a strap fifteen feet below him. His bunny boots scraped the white powder just as he stalled his ram air parachute and settled standing up into three feet of snow. The rest of the team came down silently next to and behind him, all within forty feet. "Everybody tether yourselves to the man in front of and behind you. Use four arm spans and throw in two or three brake knots. Order of march will be Jon, Angie, me, Spooge, Roadkill, and Reaper," Boss transmitted.

Jon quickly attached his snowshoes to his white Mickey Mouse boots and shouldered his pack. He opened his ATAK-equipped tablet to study the best route to pursue the mercs.

Angie shuffled up next to Jon on his snowshoes and grabbed Jon's rope. He tied three brake knots in the climbing rope before attaching one end to the large rescue carabiner on Jon's chest rig and the other end to his own. Without a word, he walked back and repeated the process with Boss. Within a couple of minutes, everyone was up on their snowshoes and connected in line every eight yards or so.

"Is everyone set?" Boss asked. He looked up and down the line and received five thumbs up. "Okay, Jon step off. Use the terrain for cover and concealment wherever possible."

"Wilco," Jon replied before shuffling up the slope toward the crest. The snowshoes and adjustable snowshoe poles they picked up at Malmstrom made traveling much easier than post-holing through the three-foot-deep snow. As they got closer to their targets, they would have to put away the poles. A half-hour later, Jon transmitted softly, "The snow is getting heavier. I'm having trouble seeing more than ten meters even with my goggles."

"Take your time, Jon. We don't want to walk into an ambush," Boss replied.

"Any chance of getting ISR up tonight?" Roadkill asked.

"Negative. Ghost 11 and the ISR platforms are all grounded until the blizzard passes," Boss replied between labored breaths. "Every once in a while, one of our EO sats gets glimpses of our target crossing Agassiz Glacier. They're at least a couple of miles ahead of us."

Jon made his way across the glacier's snowfield for about 200 meters. He was between Kintla Peak and Mount Peabody when the snow beneath him disintegrated to form a jagged thirty-foot-wide hole.

***

"Jon!" Angie shouted as his best friend disappeared. He was immediately yanked off his feet and pulled quickly headfirst toward the crevasse. He let go of his snowshoe poles and tried frantically to grab his ice axe off his pack. He lurched to a stop hanging upside down with his body from the waist down in the crevasse facing Jon.

"Hold on, Angie. We're getting anchored in and then I'll crawl out to you," Boss transmitted. Boss and the other three kicked off their snowshoes and tamped their legs down into the deep snow. They leaned back to increase their tension on the rope.

Before Angie could reply he slipped another foot into the hole. He made eye contact with Jon in time to see Jon's Ka-Bar cut the rope. "No, Jonny!" Angie shouted as Jon disappeared into the deep dark hole. Angie rushed to pull a green chemlight from his cargo pocket. He snapped it and dropped it into the hole. It never hit bottom. Instead, it fell until the inky black enveloped it.

"What the Hell happened?" Boss transmitted as the team pulled Angie up out of and away from the hole.

Angie choked back a sob and wiped his tears before replying, "The crazy bastard cut his rope! I have to find him!" He stood up, turned back toward the hole, and stepped off with determination. Boss tackled him and held him down long enough for Roadkill to arrive and reinforce him. "Let go!" Angie shouted.

"Wait a minute dammit. We'll do this the smart way. Spooge, get your ass up here with the climbing rope and we'll lower Angie into the hole," Boss ordered.

"Roger that, Boss," Spooge replied.

"Can we let you go now, Angie?" Boss asked.

"Yes, sir," Angie replied.

Five minutes later, Angie was being lowered into the hole. He had descended 30 feet when he transmitted, "Stop here." The team held him in position. "It's so dark my goggles aren't working very well. I can hear water rushing by below me. I'm going to turn my light on. He looked at the rock and ice walls around him. There's no sign of Jon, no blood or equipment left behind." He dropped a white chemlight into the water. "There's a deep creek ten feet below me. It's moving fast. He must have been swept away. Pull me up." In less than a minute he was pulled up over the edge of the hole and onto the snow. He stood before Boss and said, "We have to go after him."

"I'm sorry, Angie, but you know that's impossible," Boss said as he looked at his watch. "He's already been in ice-cold water for seven or eight minutes. He can't hold his breath that long and we have no idea if or where he may have resurfaced. He's dead, Angie. There is no other possible outcome. Now, we have a mission to complete, or tens of millions of people will be murdered. Are you hearing me?" Boss asked.

"Yes, sir," Angie said. He was heartbroken. He loved Jon like a brother, but he knew Boss was right. "I don't know how I'm going to tell Jon's fiancée, Sarah," Angie said.

"You're not. That's my job," Boss said firmly, before turning to the others. "New order of march, Spooge, Angie, me, Roadkill, and Reaper."

CHAPTER 5

Michael leaned over and shined his light on the dying man at the edge of the creek. "Leave him be. He's mine," a disembodied voice said from the darkness.

"No, you can't have him. God loves this man and says he is worthy of redemption," Michael replied.

"Ridiculous! He has murdered over a hundred people!" the voice complained. "He is definitely mine!"

"No, he has killed in defense of the weak and innocent. He is a protector, but you can try to take him if you like," Michael taunted him with a smile. The voice did not respond. "That's what I thought. You've never been one for a fair fight," Michael replied as he threw the man over his shoulder before hurrying off into the trees.

"My day will come!" the voice warned.

"Not likely," Michael scoffed at the liar, not bothering to look back at him.

CHAPTER 6

0245, DECEMBER 25, DAY 2,
EMERGENCY SNOW SHELTER,
GLACIER NATIONAL PARK, MONTANA

Jon woke up on his left side curled up in a ball shivering. He had never been this cold in his life, not even during Hell Week. He opened his eyes and looked around. Yellow light flickered off the frozen white wall a foot from his face. He could tell he was in a sleeping bag inside an igloo or something similar. He was on a snow shelf facing the wall. Despite his situation, he felt an overwhelming sense of love and protection.

"Merry Christmas, Jon. Welcome back to the living. How do you feel?" a strong male voice asked him from behind.

Who is that? How does he know my name? Jon thought. He took several deep breaths before he tried to roll over. On his fourth attempt, he was able to flip over to his right side. Five feet away on the other side of a small fire he saw an imposing man sitting on the other ice shelf tending the flames with a stick.

"CCCold," was all Jon could say.

"I'm sorry about that, but I didn't think you'd want to wake up in a sleeping bag cuddled up with me," the man said with a smile.

At that moment Jon realized he was naked. "WWWhere are my clothes?" Jon asked.

The man pointed his stick at the wall beyond Jon's feet. "They're hanging on the line to dry. You've been out for a while so they're almost ready."

Jon looked the man over. He had long wild black hair with streaks of gray and a matching beard and mustache. He appeared old and war-weary, but also still fully capable and committed. His broad muscular shoulders were barely contained inside a National Parks Service Park Ranger uniform. "WWWho are you?" Jon asked.

"My name is Michael, but you can call me Mike," he said as he poked the fire. His shirt sleeves were rolled up to below his elbows displaying intricate tattoos wrapped around his huge forearms. The tats depicted a massive battle being fought between angels and demons.

"NNNice tats," Jon said.

Mike looked them over and said, "I got these a long time ago during my intemperate youth." He reached into his pack with his right hand and pulled out two large thermos bottles. "How about some stew and hot cocoa to warm you up?" Mike asked as he poured them into the cups and handed them over the flames to Jon.

Jon sat up with the bottom of the sleeping bag dangling off the shelf. "Thank you," he said before he brought his mouth to the lip of the steaming cup to test the temperature of the stew. It was so hot he had to blow on it. "Is this Zurek?" Jon asked.

"Yes. I came across it ages ago in Poland," Mike replied.

Jon nodded before saying, "I thought so. I had some a while back." He blew on a spoonful for a few seconds and put it in his mouth. He didn't realize how hungry he really was. *I guess almost dying will do that to you,* he thought. Mike chuckled and nodded.

"What's so funny?" Jon asked between mouthfuls. The Zurek was quickly warming him up, almost like a magic potion.

"Oh, it was nothing," Mike replied.

Jon swallowed and asked, "So how did I get here?"

"My partner, Raphael, and I were in the Numa Ridge Lookout Tower watching your team pursue Devilin's gang across the glacier when you fell in the crevasse. We call it the Devil's Hole. We knew the water rushing off the glacier that you fell into would flow into the Akokala Creek and about where it would dump you out. You held your breath for four minutes. That's pretty good, even for a SEAL. I found you passed out on the creek bank about a mile downhill from where you went in. I brought you back here to warm up while Raphael continued to shadow Devilin's gang and your team. After you're feeling better, I'll take you out in front of Devilin so you can cut him off," Mike explained.

Jon stopped eating and gave him the side-eye. "How do you know so much about me and why I'm here? None of this makes sense. How did you get me to this snow shelter and how long did it take you to build it, or do you just have them built all around the park just in case a dumb-ass like me needs to be rescued? How come you're not wet? How come you were out there in the middle of a massive blizzard?" Jon asked.

"We all have bosses, Jon. Your boss put you out there in the middle of a blizzard to chase down and kill a mad scientist bent on annihilating millions of people just to see if he can. My boss put me out there to look after you so you and your boys can make sure that doesn't happen," Mike replied.

"Where's my radio? I need to call my team," Jon said as he started looking around the small snow cave.

Mike pointed to Jon's left and said, "It's still on your plate carrier."

Jon dragged it closer to him, wincing in pain. His fingers were still sore from being so cold. "Charlie 1, this is Charlie 4, over," Jon transmitted. There was no answer. He repeated the call. Still nothing. "Charlie Team, this is Charlie 4. Does anyone hear me, over." He pulled the radio out of its holder and opened the battery compartment. The battery was wet. He held it over the fire and shook the water off.

Mike pulled a tan and brown Middle Eastern shemagh from his back pocket and said, "Here you go," before handing it to Jon.

Jon looked it over. The camouflage pattern was actually Bible verses. He read one to himself, *Revelation 12:7-9: Then war broke out in heaven. Michael and his angels fought against the dragon, and the dragon and his angels fought back. But he was not strong enough, and they lost their place in heaven.* Jon looked up at Michael. He smiled back. Jon wiped the battery and radio dry before putting the battery back in the radio and giving Michael's scarf back to him. He called Boss and the team several more times, but the radio was tango uniform. "Can I borrow your radio?" he asked Michael.

"Sure, but I don't think they're compatible. Our radios aren't encrypted," Michael replied as he handed over his radio.

Jon tried several times anyway before giving the radio back. "What agency do you work for, because you're sure not a park ranger?" Jon asked.

"Why not? If you can be a marshal, I can be a park ranger. See, I have a badge, gun, and everything," Mike smiled as he motioned at all the ranger accouterments lying around him. "Come on. Finish your stew and cocoa and we'll go get these hombres," Mike said as he reached over and squeezed the cuff of Jon's trouser leg, "Your clothes are dry."

"Everything you know about me and Devilin is classified. There's no way you could get that information," Jon pushed some more.

"Trust me, Jon, my clearance is higher than yours, much higher," Mike explained. "And thank you for what you did for Sister Joan and the orphans of Saint Michael's. Your conduct was truly selfless and admirable. My boss was very pleased with you, and I was impressed."

"How did you find out about that?" Jon asked.

Mike smiled and said, "It was on TV." Jon remembered Russian motorists had videoed him and Angie attacking the Chechen military convoy. "I even found one of your wanted posters on the internet."

"I wiped out a platoon of men that day," Jon said with regret.

"No, Jon. You saved your goddaughter and 91 orphans from horrible deaths at the hands of truly evil men. If you have doubts, if you are looking for absolution, I can tell you, you have it. God loves you, Jon. While you do his work you will wear his armor and tonight, he wants you to stop these evil men even if you have to kill them," Mike replied.

"God is issuing death warrants now?" Jon asked.

"Yes, he is. He always has. No life ends without his nod. He loves his children but sometimes they must be disciplined. You'll understand better when Sarah and you have your own children," Mike replied. He could tell Jon was still dubious. "Do you believe in God, Jon, I mean really believe? Not just on Christmas and Easter? I thought you did with all the praying you do when you're getting shot at or someone you love is in danger. I've lost count of the number of times you've prayed to God to take your life and spare someone else. Even tonight you were praying your tail off while you were underwater."

Jon teared up as he swallowed hard and nodded, "Yes."

"Jon, you have been crashing headfirst through life like you have a death wish. It's not your time. You may not understand it, but you're doing God's will. You are where he wants you to be and he will decide when to call you home," Mike said, "But you could ease up on the f-bombs."

Mike's radio came alive. "Mike, this is Gabriel, over."

Mike keyed the microphone clipped to his shirt. "Go ahead, Gabe."

"Raphael just called in. Devilin is on the Agassiz Glacier between Kintla Peak and Mount Peabody," Gabriel replied.

"What about Charlie Team?" Mike asked.

"They lost about fifteen minutes looking for Jonathan after he fell into the Devil's Hole, but they're on Devilin's trail now and gaining ground. The blizzard is getting worse," Gabriel transmitted.

"Understood. We'll head out in about ten minutes to arc around and get in front of them," Mike transmitted. He said to

Jon, "Okay, break's over. Get dressed and we'll get after them." Jon watched as Mike leaned his stick against the snow shelf next to his leg as he began closing his pack and putting on his cold-weather gear. The next time he looked, the stick wasn't a stick anymore. It was a sword with flames engraved on the thick black blade. *Holy shit! That's Saint Michael's flaming sword!* Jon thought. Mike turned to look at Jon as if he heard his thoughts, picked up his sword, and slid it into the scabbard on his left hip. Jon locked eyes with him and said, "You're Michael the Archangel."

"Finally figuring that out, huh, Jon," Michael replied. "Come on, finish getting dressed."

Jon threw his blouse over his trousers and began buttoning it up, "Ah, I remember from Sunday School you lent your sword to Joshua in the Battle of Jericho. Do you mind if I borrow it for a while?" Jon asked.

"Yeah, well, you ain't Joshua. You might hurt yourself. Besides, you seem to do pretty well with your Ka-Bar already," Michael replied as he bent over to leave the shelter. Jon rushed through putting his coat, gloves, balaclava, and helmet on. Jon went down on all fours as he crawled through the snow shelter's small opening out into the blizzard. They trudged through the snow to Michael's top-of-the-line Red Polaris snowmobile. Mike brushed the snow off the seat with his arm.

"Aren't snowmobiles outlawed in the Park?" Jon asked.

"I got a waiver from the original developer of the Park," Michael replied as he straddled the machine. "Let's go."

Jon climbed aboard and put his arms around Michael. He felt like he was holding onto a granite statue wrapped in Gortex. "So does this mean I'm an angel, now?" Jon asked as the snowmobile accelerated forward.

Mike laughed and shouted, "No!" over his shoulder, "Maybe a minion, yeah, you're a minion, that's it!"

Jon nodded his head and said, "God's minion! Cool! I'll take it!" Seconds later it occurred to him, *I'm riding bitch into battle behind Michael the Archangel.*

CHAPTER 7

Spooge struggled against a twenty-knot headwind with his head down trying to see the snowshoe trail left by Devilin's goons. He and the rest of Charlie Team were still tethered together as they headed north and down slope across Agassiz Glacier. They were solemn but determined to catch and eliminate Devilin and his mercs. They had reluctantly accepted the fact that Jon was dead, and his body might never be recovered. All except Angie. He still held on to a sliver of hope. After they killed Devilin he'd go find Jon on his own if necessary.

"Boss, the snow is blowing so hard I might walk into these assholes before I see them," Spooge transmitted over his secure team radio.

"Yeah, I know, but the stakes are too high to let them get away from us. Keep going," Boss replied. What he left unsaid, that everyone knew, was on this mission they were all expendable. They might have to take one for the team. They would Charlie Mike until the last man fell face-first into the snow.

Spooge responded with two clicks from his radio. He took several steps before he felt a slight click under his left snowshoe. He realized immediately it was some sort of pressure-activated anti-personnel mine, but it exploded before he could react, throwing his mangled left leg up into the air causing him to cartwheel backward, landing on his face. It was a Russian PMN-4 anti-personnel mine. Powerful enough to destroy a leg, while leaving the victim incapacitated. The nauseating pain made him scream uncontrollably. Without help, he would bleed out.

Angie unclipped his tether and ran to him as fast as he could on his snowshoes as he transmitted, "Everyone get off the trail!" Angie stopped about six feet short of Spooge and pulled him toward him and away from the trail with their safety line. Angie dropped to his knees and released Spooge's pack before rolling him over. He saw green blood surging out of a massive wound below the knee. The left boot was still attached to Spooge's leg by a few strands of skin and muscle. A couple of inches of bone were missing. He flashed back, momentarily, to when he almost lost his own leg in Sumatra. *Thank you, God, for sending Jon to save me,* he thought. Angie took the tourniquet from Spooge's chest rig and applied it as far down from the knee as he could. Hopefully, he would be able to jog on a prosthesis in a year or so if he was, somehow, able to get off the glacier tonight.

The tourniquet hurt almost as much as his shattered leg. "Oh Lord Jesus, please help me! Angie, I'm dying!" Spooge cried out.

"I got you, Tommy! Stop whining! I stopped the bleeding! You're going to live!" He refused to call a dying man, Spooge. "Here, keep this in your mouth and suck on it!" Angie yelled into his ear before pushing a Fentanyl Citrate lollipop between his teeth.

"Roadkill, Reaper, set up security. We don't want those bastards attacking us while we treat, Spooge," Angie and Spooge heard Boss transmit over the team radio. Angie was opening a splint to put Spooge's leg back together when Boss appeared out of the blinding snow. He looked down at the badly mangled leg. *He won't make it through the night on this glacier,* he thought. "Hang on, Spooge!" Boss yelled as he squeezed his shoulder. He stepped back and grabbed Angie's arm before leaning in to talk quietly into Angie's ear, "How bad is he?"

Angie turned to talk into Boss's ear, "I stopped the bleeding for now with a tourniquet, but we need to get him to a hospital ASAP or he'll die."

Boss looked up to the sky, but all he saw through his GPNVGs was heavy snow whipping around him in the wind. *God, if you're up there, Tommy could really use your help. He's a good kid. He doesn't deserve this. Me for sure, but not him,* Boss prayed. He reached under his goggles to wipe his eyes. He cleared his throat, "I'll call Ghost 11, but I doubt if they can come out in this mess," he said. Boss switched frequencies and transmitted, "Ghost 11, this is Charlie 1, over."

A reply came immediately, "Charlie 1, go for Ghost 11." It was Ghost 11 actual, the pilot in command or PC, retired Army Night Stalker, CW5 Pat Minx, callsign Deacon.

Boss gave Deacon an abbreviated nine-line brief, "Ghost 11, I have one, urgent-surgical, traumatic amputation below the knee on Agassiz Glacier, grid coordinates 48.9315 north, 114.1586 west. We'll mark our location with an IR strobe. Elevation 7,800'. Enemy unit unknown distance to the north, over."

"Ghost 11 copies all. Keep him alive. We're inbound. ETA twenty-five mikes," Deacon replied.

***

Deacon opened the right cockpit door to the MH-60 DAP Black Hawk, grabbed his aviation armor and survival vest off his armored seat, and shouted, "Get the hangar doors open! We're launching!"

The airport manager ran out of the hangar's office and yelled as he shook his head, "You guys can't take off. The airport's closed because of the blizzard."

Deacon grabbed the larger man by the collar of his coat and shouted, "We have a man on the glacier with his leg blown off! We're goin'! Open the dad-gum doors right now!" He could knock this guy out with one punch without blinking, but he couldn't actually utter a real curse word. It just wasn't in him.

The manager turned and ran to the wall at the edge of the hangar door and pressed the button to open them. The doors slowly opened fifteen feet and crunched to a stop. Deacon wasn't waiting. He and his copilot, Willi, began the start sequence on the first engine and the rotor blades started to turn inside the hangar. The left gunner stood in front of the cockpit manning the fire extinguisher.

The manager ran to the cockpit and shouted, "The doors are frozen!"

Deacon nodded and threw him a thumbs up and then transmitted over his intercom system or ICS to his crew chief, "Chuck, I don't care what it takes. Get those doors open right dang now!"

Chuck could tell Deacon was pissed. He didn't start throwing dangs and dad-gums around until he was ready to tear shit up. If he said son of a biscuit someone might get hurt. "Roger that," Chuck replied before disconnecting his ICS long cord and dropping it on his seat.

"Joe, walk around the helicopter one more time and pull the chocks," Deacon ordered.

Chuck jogged over to the airport's FBO truck parked in the corner and started it up. He drove over to the other corner where the manager was mashing on the hangar door button. Chuck shouted through the open truck window, "Just keep the button depressed and I'll take care of the rest."

"The helicopter is clear, and the chocks are inside," Joe stated after he climbed into the helicopter through his left gunner's window.

Chuck drove along the inside of the door until he came to the opening. He turned sharply to the left and then back to the right to position the front bumper of the truck against the far hangar door. He moved the truck forward until he felt the door resist and then he steadily pressed down on the accelerator until the door moaned loudly in complaint before begrudgingly sliding back. The last twenty feet sounded like the door was dragging the USS Teddy Roosevelt's anchor chain across the floor. The other door surrendered immediately and opened of its own accord. Chuck parked in the far corner and ran back to the chopper. He climbed in through his gunner's window and connected his ICS before transmitting, "All set in back."

"Well done, Chuck. Let's get the heck out of here," Deacon said before ground taxiing out of the hangar onto the concrete ramp.

Willi scanned the instrument panel and said, "Gauges are green," before giving Deacon a thumbs up.

"Coming up," Boss said before he performed an instrument take-off into the raging blizzard.

"Clear up and left," Joe said.

"Clear up and right," Chuck said.

***

Boss checked the time on his chest-mounted ATAK tablet. Twenty minutes had passed since he requested the medivac. He looked up to the sky again. The weather still looked like shit. If anything, it had gotten worse, but he trusted Deacon to do the impossible. If he said he was coming, you could bank on it. "Your ride will be here any minute, Spooge. A half an hour from now you'll take a nap in the ER and wake up in a warm bed with a PCA button in your hand," Boss said confidently. The Patient-Controlled Analgesia or PCA pump allowed patients to self-administer pain medication in the hospital. Then Boss's thoughts went back to the mission. *I haven't seen Devilin or his mercs yet and I'm already down two good men. That's a 33% casualty rate. In the military, my team would be considered combat ineffective. I have four guys against what? At least ten vicious mercs. After this one, maybe it's time to retire to the fishing boat in Boca*, he thought.

***

The fentanyl lollipops had helped curb the excruciating pain. Spooge looked up at Boss's back as he stood guard over him. "Boss, do you think I can come back from this?" Spooge asked.

Boss glanced back at him. "We all know crazy assholes who have lost a foot and made their way back to operate again. So, yeah, I do. It'll be the hardest thing you've ever done, but if you want it bad enough you can make it back to the team," Boss said truthfully. "Or you could just say screw it and take the money and run."

"Charlie 1, this is Ghost 11, over," Deacon transmitted.

"Go for Charlie 1," Boss replied.

"We're five minutes out. Keep your heads down. I'm going to offset about thirty feet up slope from you. When you hear us turn on your strobe," Deacon transmitted.

"Charlie copies all. Thanks, brother," Boss replied. He went down to one knee and shouted over the howling blizzard swirling around him, "Did you hear that Spooge? It won't be long now!"

Spooge was semi-conscious. He knew he shouldn't go to sleep, but he wanted to more than anything right now. He summoned enough strength to nod and raise his thumb.

"Here's one more for the road, Tommy," Angie shouted into his ear as he put another fentanyl lollipop into his mouth. Angie keyed his team radio and transmitted, "Chuck, are you up?"

"Affirmative, Angie," he replied.

"Tommy is semi-conscious. I just gave him a third lollipop. The tourniquet is working but I estimate he lost about two liters of blood. I started an IV. Make sure you guys keep him warm," Angie transmitted.

"Will do," Chuck replied.

Two minutes later, Boss heard the Black Hawk's engines and rotor blades fighting their way through the roaring blizzard. Thankfully, temperatures had been zero or below in the mountains, so Deacon didn't have to worry about ice forming on his helicopter. Visibility was effectively zero. He had been flying solely on instruments since taking off from the airport.

Boss activated the IR strobe attached to his helmet before dropping to his knees again and opened his white camo smock. He held it open as wide as he could and covered Spooge and Angie. He knew the helo would generate a tornado of sub-zero swirling snow when it landed, and he wanted to block as much of it as he could.

***

Landing checks complete," Willi said as he held his right thumb in front of the instrument panel.

"Okay, I'm going to fly us down to the surface on instruments. Willi, back me up on instruments but keep scanning outside. Set your rad alt to fifty feet. I'll do the same. You guys in back keep your heads outside and keep checking our tail. If you don't like something, tell me to go around," Deacon said over the ICS. He lowered the collective and pulled back on the cyclic to decrease his airspeed and stay 100 feet above the snow-covered surface. After he slowed to 10 knots he checked his GPS again. He was approaching his landing zone. He came to a hover and pointed the nose to the south.

Silent green tracers flew by the helicopter randomly on both sides. "Contact six o'clock!" Joe called out over the ICS.

Deacon replied calmly, "Return fire as appropriate." His rotor blade tips were spinning at 100% Nr, approximately 476 mph. He was more concerned with bumping them into a granite cloud than getting hit with a golden BB.

Joe returned fire with his M134 minigun. The M134 was an American-made 7.62×51mm NATO six-barreled Gatling-style machine gun with a variable 2,000 to 6,000 rounds per minute rate of fire. It tended to win most arguments. Joe couldn't see if he hit anything, but the incoming tracers definitely stopped. "Anything more to say?" he asked quietly for his own benefit, "Yeah, that's what I thought."

Deacon adjusted a little to the left and then said, "Coming down." He lowered the collective slightly to start a descent. He tried to envision gently coming down through an elevator shaft. He caught himself white-knuckling the controls and forced himself to ease up on his grip.

"Seventy feet," Willi called out.

"Roger," Deacon said with his Chuck Yeager voice. He continued cross-checking his vertical speed indicator, heading, airspeed indicator, and GPS.

"Sixty feet, airspeed zero," Willi called.

"I see a strobe beneath us bleeding through the blowing snow," Chuck reported.

"Fifty feet, airspeed zero," Willi said as the warning light on the rad alt lit up.

"Roger. Lower the rad alt bug to ten feet," Deacon said.

"Rad alt set to ten feet on the left side," Willi replied.

"The IR strobe is getting brighter," Chuck advised.

"Thirty feet, airspeed zero," Willi advised. He moved his hands closer to the controls just in case he had to take over. "Twenty feet," Willi called out.

"Hold your descent!" Chuck called abruptly. Deacon raised the collective. "You're directly over three men from Charlie Team. Slide left thirty feet." Deacon did as directed. "Okay, they're clear. You're clear to descend," Chuck said.

"Coming down," Deacon replied.

"Ten feet," Willi called.

"Clear right and below," Chuck said.

"Clear left and below," Joe said.

The snowshoe attached to the tailwheel touched down sinking five inches into the snow followed by the left main mount and then the right. Charlie Team quickly carried Spooge over the crusty snow to the open cabin door and Chuck and Joe pulled him inside and began securing him.

Boss stepped forward to Deacon's door and opened it. "For a second there I thought you were going to land on top of us!" he yelled over the storm.

"I couldn't see a darn thing! Why didn't you say something?" Deacon asked.

Boss smiled, "You're the friggin' pilot! Hey, thanks for comin'! I don't think I could bear to lose any more people tonight!" Boss replied as they shook hands.

"After we get Tommy to the ER, we'll go back to the airport to refuel and check the chopper for holes. Then we'll come back out here and orbit the area just in case you need us. Maybe I'll let Willi fly for a while. He already thinks I'm a stick hog," Deacon said.

"It's about time. I have the controls," Willi replied.

CHAPTER 8

Mike and Jon were making good time cruising up the snow-covered trail next to frozen Akokala Creek.

"How much longer?" Jon shouted in his ear.

"Not long. We'll be on Agassiz Glacier in a couple of minutes," Michael replied.

Michael's radio crackled to life. "Michael, this is Gabriel, over."

"Go ahead Gabe," Michael transmitted back to him.

"Raphael relayed, that Jon's teammate, Thomas, stepped on a mine hidden along the trail on the glacier. His left leg was badly damaged, but his team leader was able to call in a helicopter to medivac him to the hospital," Gabe replied.

"Damn, ask him about the rest of the team," Jon said.

Before Michael could respond, Gabriel transmitted, "Everyone else is fine."

"Thanks, Gabe, out," Michael replied as he slowed to a stop.

"Why are we stopping?" Jon asked.

"There's a cottonwood tree lying across the trail. Stay here. I'll move it," Michael said. He trudged through the thigh-high snow to the tree, raised his sword over his head with both hands, and drove it through the six-foot diameter tree with one stroke. He moved to the right fifteen feet and repeated the process. He sheathed his sword, grabbed the fifteen-foot-long log with both arms and tossed it aside. He walked back to the snowmobile.

Before Michael could get on Jon pointed and said, "What the Hell is that?" What appeared to be a ten-foot-tall flaming Sasquatch holding a longsword and black shield emblazoned with an inverted pentagram was standing on the trail in the opening Michael had just created. Jon stood up on the snowmobile and fired several bursts into the monster.

Mike grabbed Jon's SAW by its red-hot barrel and forced Jon to lower it, "Save your ammo. That's the Great Deceiver, again. I'll deal with him. Take the snowmobile and show your team the way to intercept Devilin. I programmed the route into your ATAK tablet when you were sleeping," Michael said. He turned in time to see Satan spewing a wall of flames toward him and Jon. He laughed and shouted, "Begone foul demon!" as he ran headlong into the flames while waving his sword over his head. Jon was transfixed by the sight. Michael grabbed Satan's shield and flung it aside. Satan countered by swinging his longsword at Michael's neck. Michael parried with his sword and punched the devil in the face knocking him onto his back. Michael sheathed his blade and grabbed Satan by his right ankle. He spun in a circle several times while holding Satan's leg like a discus thrower before launching him 200 feet beyond frozen Akokala Creek into the snow-covered south slope below Kintla Peak.

"Jon, get out of here! I got this!" the happy warrior, Michael, shouted before sprinting away into the trees. Seconds later, Jon saw him appear briefly above the trees as he long jumped the frozen creek.

I must be high or something. Maybe the guys rescued me from the creek and I'm still dreaming. Angie must have pumped me up with morphine. I really like morphine, Jon thought. "Wait a minute," he said to himself as he opened his ATAK and found the GPS route labeled Ambush Site Route. *How did this route get in my tablet? Maybe it's also part of the dream.* He started the snowmobile and accelerated up the trail. *At least it's a really cool dream,* he thought.

***

Fifteen minutes later, Jon was fighting the blizzard as he followed the route Michael gave him. It led him around the edge of the glacier. Jon figured it was an attempt to avoid more crevasses, kind of like a safe route through a minefield. The blizzard let up enough for Jon to see a hundred feet or so in front of him. He stopped to scan the area through his GPNVGs for any man-made trails. The snow-covered landscape in front of him as far as he could see was pristine. There was no sign of Devilin or his goons. Either he was already in front of them, or they were following another path. He was about to restart the snowmobile when he felt the ground shake under him. It wasn't like before when the crevasse swallowed him. This was more like something was below the ice fighting to get out, but he knew that was crazy.

Suddenly, he heard thunderous crashes emanating from the ice beneath the five-foot-deep layer of snow. Snow and ice flew into the air in five-story tall geysers. One by one three mastodons climbed onto the surface. They trumpeted back and forth angrily before charging each other to tussle on their rear legs. They were either establishing a pecking order or settling old grievances. Then they saw Jon and his snowmobile. They turned and charged him in unison.

"Aw shit!" he shouted as he stood up above the snowmobile and fired a burst from his short-barreled M249 SAW into the lead bull's forehead. He saw the green tracers bounce off in all directions. If anything, the 5.56 NATO rounds just pissed him off. The big bull was on Jon instantly. He knocked Jon off the snowmobile with his trunk and used his massive forehead to pound Jon into the snow. After three blows he wrapped his trunk around Jon and flung him fifty feet across the glacier. Jon sat up and fired two more long bursts into the leader, this time aiming for his legs and torso. Jon felt sore from being stomped and tossed around but not like anything was broken or he was going to die. *I should be dead. How am I still fighting,* he wondered. Then he remembered what Mike said, while you do his work you will wear his armor. He fired another couple of bursts into the big bull, this time the bull faltered and fell over. The other two poked and prodded him, encouraging him to get up.

Jon took the opportunity to run for the snowmobile. He quickly started the engine, spun the machine around 180°, and sped back from where he came. "Mike! A little help here!" Jon shouted as the two remaining mastodons pursued him. He heard another thunderous crack and then screams behind him. He turned in time to see the final mastodon fall into a newly formed crevasse. He spun the tail around and stopped. He heard a rumbling coming from above and to his left. A humongous avalanche was roaring down from Kintla Peak. "Hell Yeah! Thanks, Mike!" he shouted as he accelerated south to get out of its path.

CHAPTER 9

"How's it looking up there, Angie?" Boss asked over the team radio. Angie was now on point. The blizzard was worse than before. Boss couldn't see him on the other end of the tether.

"I'm as blind as a one-eyed joey sitting in mama's pouch, mate. It's zero vis up here. I'm six feet off the trail and the snow is falling so fast it's almost obliterated the snowshoe trail," Angie replied before being yanked back off his feet to be dragged back the way he came. He knew instantly another crevasse had opened up and at least one man had fallen in. He let go of his snowshoe poles and grabbed his ice axe. He swung it into the snow. It slowed his pace and allowed his body to turn 180°. "I'm going in!" he shouted as his legs and his torso went over the side. He drove his axe into the snow again and it stopped his movement just as his chest went over the side. He had no idea how deep the hole was or how bad off Boss was at the other end of the rope.

"Boss, can you hear me!" he shouted. He was holding onto the axe handle with both hands. He didn't dare let either one of them go but he couldn't dangle there on the edge of the abyss much longer. His arms were already quivering from the strain. He contemplated letting go with his left hand in order to reach his knife to cut the tether. He knew his weight would eventually cause Roadkill and Reaper to be pulled into the crevasse with Boss and him. Before he acted Boss's weight disappeared from the line. He must have cut Angie loose to give him a chance at life.

***

"Boss, hang on! We're coming!" Roadkill transmitted over the team radio.

"Negative! Hold your ground! I'm hanging upside down in another crevasse," he transmitted. "Angie, can you hear me, over," Boss transmitted over the team radio. He tried several more times to no avail. "Angie, can you hear me!" He shouted across the abyss. There was no reply. Boss was being held about five feet from the edge of the crevasse by Angie's end of the tether. He drew his knife and cut the tether between him and Angie. Boss immediately slammed into the side of the icy rock wall. He groaned in pain as the wind was knocked out of him.

"Are you okay, Boss? We felt some weight drop off the line," Roadkill transmitted.

"Yeah, Angie's end of the tether was above me, but he was being pulled into the hole from the other side, so I cut the line. I'm hoping he wasn't over the edge yet. Here's the plan. One at a time, Reaper, you go first. Dig out a hole in the snow to drop your pack in. The snow must be four or five feet deep by now. Then hook a line to it and bury it in as much snow as you can. Pack it down real good to anchor it. After you're done, Roadkill, you do the same. Then Reaper, keep the tension on the line as you pull yourself to Roadkill. After you are anchored together, rest your arms for a few minutes. Then when you're ready you can start pulling me up," Boss transmitted.

***

Only minutes had passed, but they felt like hours. Angie was almost out of strength and ideas.

"Angie, can you hear me, over," Angie heard over his radio as Boss transmitted.

The pain extending from his fingertips to below his shoulder blades was excruciating. Sweat poured from his head, soaking his white balaclava. *Lord, please, help me! I don't think I can bear much more of this! I know I've not been a good Christian at times, but I've tried to do the right thing when I could,* he prayed. The axe handle slowly slipped from his grasp. His eyes went wide behind his clear-eye pro and GPNVGs before he closed them again. He always assumed he would take a round to his grape or be blown up in combat, not fall into a frozen abyss. It was an ignoble way to die, bloody embarrassing. *Lord, please don't let me die like this,* he prayed.

"I got you, brother!" Jon shouted over the blizzard as he straddled the axe blade and grabbed Angie's wrists.

Angie continued to cling to the handle. "You're dead, mate! You can't help me anymore!" Angie shouted back.

"Angie, open your eyes! It's me! You're okay! Let go of the axe!" Jon shouted.

"Jonny," Angie said as his eyes opened and he released his grip. "You're dead, mate. I saw you die."

"Yeah, well, I got better," Jon replied. Jon pulled Angie's hands about a foot further away from the edge. One hand at a time, he moved his grip to the drag handle on the back of Angie's plate carrier. He pulled again, this time bringing Angie's waist over the edge. He kicked the ice axe out of the way and allowed himself to settle back into the snow pulling Angie with him. Jon grabbed Angie by his gun belt and pulled him up until they were face to face lying in the snow.

"You're not going to kiss me, are you, mate?" Angie said, barely able to crack a smile.

"You wish. I'd be a step up after the butter-faced hoes you've been dating," Jon replied.

Turning serious, Angie asked, "Jonny, how are you alive? I saw you fall. There was an ice-cold river rushing by under that crevasse."

"You won't believe this, but I held my breath for four minutes under the ice. Finally, the frozen creek dumped me out a mile down slope. Then this park ranger named Mike found me and carried me to a snow shelter he dug out of the snow. He dried my clothes and warmed me up. He kept saying stuff that he had no way of knowing about me and our mission. Slowly as I regained my senses, I figured out he wasn't a park ranger. He's actually Saint Michael the Archangel and he knew all about…" Jon said before being interrupted.

"Hang on, mate! Saint Michael! That's bloody ridiculous!" Angie was dubious.

"I'm serious, Angie. I saw him fighting with Satan just a little while ago. He appeared as a giant flaming Sasquatch. He had a big black shield with an upside-down pentagram and a longsword that was taller than you. Satan really wants to get a hold of me for some reason. He was willing to fight Mike to get me."

"You do have an uncanny ability to piss people off," Angie said.

"Angie, this is Boss. Can you hear me, over?" Angie and Jon heard over Angie's radio as Boss transmitted.

"Boss, this is Angie, over," he replied.

"Thank God! What's your status!" Boss asked.

"My arms are aching from hanging in the crevasse for so long, but Jon pulled me out a minute ago," Angie replied.

"Wait, what? How can Jon be there? Did you smack your head on something?" Boss asked.

"Let me talk to him," Jon said as he keyed Angie's microphone. "Hey, Boss, it's Jon. After I fell in the water, I traveled a mile downstream underwater. A park ranger named Mike fished me out of the creek and warmed me up in an emergency snow shelter. He loaned me his snowmobile so I could catch up to you."

"Why didn't you check in with me?" Boss asked, he sounded a little pissed.

"My radio's been tango uniform since I went in the water," Jon replied.

"Understood. Are you still in the fight?" Boss asked.

"Yes, sir. 100%," Jon replied.

"Welcome back to the living, Jon," Boss transmitted.

"Thank you, sir," Jon replied.

"Okay, here's the plan. You and Angie track down Devilin's gang. If you have an opportunity to kill Devilin take it. If you can get Ranger Terrell back that would be great, but the priority must be to kill that crazy bastard. We'll worry about finding the rest of his gang another day. After Roadkill and Reaper pull me out of this damned hole, we'll work our way around the crevasse and follow you. Boss, out," he transmitted.

"Charlie 4, copies all," Jon replied. "C'mon, Angie. Let's go do some hero shit," he said as he helped Angie to his feet. Jon rubbed Angie's arms for a minute to get his blood flowing, then turned toward the snowmobile.

"Where are we going? I can't see anything in this damn blizzard," Angie asked as he followed Jon.

"Mike programmed a route into my ATAK tablet to a waypoint where we can set up an ambush for Devilin's goons," Jon said.

"You mean 2,000-year-old Saint Michael the Archangel is computer literate?" Angie asked.

"He works for the creator of the universe, so yeah, he's computer literate," Jon replied. "He convinced me he was the real deal when he grabbed Satan by his ankle and threw him 200 feet into the side of a mountain."

"So, where's the snowmobile?" Angie asked as he walked up next to Jon on his snowshoes.

"It's over here," Jon answered as he pointed into a curtain of heavy blowing snow. He looked down for tracks. Even his snowshoe tracks had been erased by new snow. He turned in a circle. "I left it right here. Mike must have taken it back for some reason," Jon said.

"Supernatural being, Saint Michael the Archangel needs a snowmobile to move around in a blizzard while he fights the devil and his demons," Angie was able to wisecrack.

"Funny," Jon said as he looked down at his ATAK tablet. "We're only 500 meters from the ambush site. We can walk it from here. C'mon," Jon said.

CHAPTER 10

Devilin was of average size, but daily prison workouts made him lean and strong. He had what Jon Smith called a soccer ninja body. He was in excellent physical condition, almost as good as when he was a young infantry lieutenant. He and his gang were heading downhill now being led by Park Ranger Stacy Terrell. She was leading them toward the beginning of frozen Agassiz Creek. It offered a clear path through the forest heading straight for the Canadian border. "How much farther to the border, Ms. Terrell?" Devilin asked through his black balaclava.

She was leading the group across the heavy snow. They didn't bother with inconsequential matters like safety lines to keep each other from disappearing into the glacier. Apparently, she didn't hear him as she kept walking. Salazar motioned to the goon walking behind her to get her attention. He shuffled up behind her and slapped her on the back of her head. She fell face-first into the snow. "Dammit!" she said angrily. She got up to her knees and asked, "What do you want this time?" as she swept snow off her balaclava.

"How much farther to the border?" Salazar shouted at her through the blizzard.

She pointed north and shouted back at him, "It's about two miles that way!"

As she turned to take a step, the deep snow in front of her exploded upward as a white snow monster emerged from below the surface. It threw her over its shoulder before running for the western tree line. She screamed for her life hoping Devilin and his men would save her. She began kicking her legs and pounding the beast's back, only stopping after she saw it was wearing snowshoes.

A rapid string of red tracers zipped from the tree line toward Devilin's men, killing two of them instantly. The others, caught in the open, dove into the deep snow for some small semblance of cover before returning fire. For the moment, they lost all interest in the monster and ranger. "We need her! Don't let her get away!" Devilin shouted with his face buried in the snow behind Salazar. Two more men rose to pursue and were immediately riddled with numerous 5.56mm NATO rounds by Angie.

"Who the Hell are you!" She shouted over the cacophony surrounding her.

"US Marshals!" Jon shouted back as he ran for a huge Cottonwood tree about ten feet from where Angie was lying behind a similar tree with Jon's SAW. Just before Jon turned behind the tree Ranger Terrell cried out in pain. Jon felt the impact flow from her body into the ceramic plate on his back. He knew she had been shot before he dropped her behind the tree. "Where are you hit, ranger?" Jon asked as he removed an Israeli battle dressing from his chest rig.

"High on my right thigh!" she shouted as she applied pressure with her gloved hands. Blood coursed out from between her fingers.

Jon ripped the vacuum-sealed bandage open with his teeth before quickly applying it to her leg, "That will stop the bleeding for now," he said as Angie continued to fire.

"Thanks! Who are you guys, really? I know some Deputy Marshals. You aren't like them!" Terrell shouted.

"We're Special Deputy US Marshals, emphasis on the special," Jon replied. He handed her his Glock 21SF and said, "Cover the right side of the tree."

"How's the sheila?" Angie asked as he reloaded the SAW. Devilin's gang's 9mm rounds continued to impact the other side of his tree.

"She took a nine mil in the thigh. The Israeli bandage stopped the bleeding. Angie, this is Ranger Stacy Terrell. Stacy, this is Angie," Jon made the introductions.

"I'm pleased to meet you, Stace," Angie said, dropping the y from her name, from behind the SAW's rear sight between bursts. "Here, put this fentanyl lollipop in your mouth. It will help with the pain," Angie said before tossing it to her.

"Thanks. I'm pleased to meet you too, Angie. Excuse me," she said before rolling over to peek around the tree. "Hey, Salazar! Show yourself maricón!" Terrell shouted. Fifteen yards away through the blizzard, she saw Salazar stick his head up above the snow.

"Don't worry, mami. I'm still here," he shouted.

Terrell quickly took aim and snapped off three rounds from Jon's Glock. The first 230-grain jacketed hollow point destroyed the bridge of Salazar's nose before mushrooming through his brain and blowing out the back of his skull. The other two rounds were wasted. "I've been wanting to do that all night," she said after rolling back behind the tree.

"Damn, sis. Are you that good with a rifle?" Jon asked.

"No, I'm better with a rifle," she replied.

"Here, take Angie's rifle," Jon said as he traded her for his pistol.

"I'm going to try to go downstream about 25 meters and envelope them. Please, try not to shoot me," Jon requested.

Angie continued to fire bursts into the snow. "I'll try, mate," he replied.

Before Jon could move, Devilin's remaining men increased their fire in an attempt to cover Devilin as he bolted for the trees on the other side of the creek.

"Cover me! I'm going after him!" Jon yelled as he hurried away on his snowshoes, heading north through the trees on his side of the creek. Twenty meters downstream he slogged across the frozen creek. Halfway across one of Devilin's men saw him and began firing at him. Jon ducked and scurried toward the trees as fast as he could. Angie recited loudly, "Die, commie, die!" while firing an eight-round burst at the man. He dropped dead and there was silence except for the blowing snow and a few men shouting back and forth in Spanish.

"What did you just say?" Terrell asked.

"Die, commie, Die!" Angie replied as he scanned the area in front of the SAW. "It's a little phrase to remind soldiers not to hold the trigger down too long and waste ammo or wear out a barrel."

"I find that oddly arousing," she said.

Angie turned to look at her and smiled from behind his bala-clava before saying, "Really." The blizzard lessened momentarily as he looked past her and saw a man emerge from the trees next to the creek 100 meters further downstream and jump. Before he could take a shot, the man disappeared from view. Angie quickly looked down at his ATAK tablet. The map showed a tightening in the contour lines representing a sharp vertical drop of fifty feet. He looked up in time to see another figure emerge from the trees and jump. "Son of a bitch!" he shouted.

"Terrell spun around behind the tree and pointed the HK416 to the north. "What is it?" she asked nervously.

"Jon just jumped off a cliff about 100 meters downstream while chasing Devilin," Angie said.

"That's insane. Does he do that sort of thing often?" she asked.

"Yeah, all the time. Stupid wanker," Angie replied in exasperation. "Hey, do you actually speak Spanish or just insults?"

"Yes, I started out in the Border Patrol," she replied.

"What are these guys saying?" Angie asked.

"They don't know what to do. They worked for Salazar and he's not talking," Terrell replied.

"Tell them they're under arrest and to stand up with their hands on their heads," Angie said.

"Okay, and then what!" She asked.

"Then I'll kill them," Angie replied.

"What? We can't do that, can we?" she asked.

"Remember what Jon said. We're Special Marshals. We don't transport prisoners or testify in court. We eliminate problems," Angie explained.

"Again, I find that oddly arousing," she said. She and Angie locked eyes for way too long and then she shouted, "Hombres, somos la policía. Manos arriba, hijos de puta." Which meant, men, we are the police. Hands up, sons of bitches.

The three remaining men stood in unison shouting Spanish curses while firing their MP5s. Angie and Terrell rolled back to take cover behind their Cottonwoods. Angie was about to return fire when he heard the unmistakable sound of multiple suppressed HK416 carbines firing on full auto. After all the guns went silent, he heard three voices shout, clear, one at a time.

Angie keyed his radio microphone and transmitted, "Boss is that you?"

"Affirmative, we're coming in," Boss replied.

Angie stood up and peeked around the huge tree looking to the south. Three men slowly materialized as they walked down the slope through the blowing snow. "It's okay, this is the other part of our team," he said to Stacy.

Boss walked over to Angie and said, "Please, tell me one of these assholes is Devilin."

"Afraid not, Boss. His gang stayed here to pin us down while he escaped over the cliff down there. Jon jumped right after him," Angie explained.

"Of course he did. Dumbass. Is he trying to kill himself twice in one night?" he asked rhetorically.

The conversation was interrupted by the muffled snap of supersonic rounds impacting flesh as Roadkill and Reaper dead-checked the cartel mercenaries scattered about the area.

He turned to Stacy. "You must be Ranger Terrell. How are you feeling?" Boss asked as he looked at the bloody bandage.

"A lot better since Jon and Angie came along," she replied.

"Any word about Tommy?" Angie asked.

"Deacon got him to the hospital alive. It's too early to tell about his foot," Boss replied.

"Our mission hasn't changed. Devilin is the priority. I'll leave Roadkill with Ms. Terrell and the rest of us will Charlie Mike." Charlie Mike meant to continue on with the mission. "Hopefully, Ghost 11 can pick her up tonight."

Roadkill and Reaper walked over to join the others. "Nice shooting Angie. That big Mexican has a hole in the back of his head you could throw a baseball through," Roadkill said.

"That wasn't me, mate. Stacy did that from back here with Jon's Glock with one shot," Angie replied.

Roadkill leaned over and held out his hand for a fist bump and said, "Good on you, ranger." She smiled and bumped his fist.

"Roadkill, you're going to stay here with Ms. Terrell. Get on the chopper with her. Do not try to follow us. Understood?" Boss asked.

"C'mon, Boss," Roadkill said.

"Stop. I saw you tweak your knee. You've been limping for hours. No bullshit. Get on the chopper. You read me?" Boss ordered.

"Yes, sir," Roadkill replied.

Angie unbuckled the straps on his pack holding his sleeping bag and opened it up, "This will keep you warm until the chopper gets here." He and Roadkill picked Terrell up and placed her in the bag. "Here's a couple more lollipops to tide you over," Angie said as he handed them to her.

She grasped his hand with both of hers and said, "Don't be a stranger, okay?"

He nodded and looked at her for a few seconds.

"Hey, lover boy. Charlie Mike," Boss said as he and Reaper shuffled away toward the cliff.

"After this is over, I'll come check on you," Angie said as he stepped back.

"Promise?" she asked.

"Yeah, Stace. I promise," Angie smiled under his balaclava, then turned to walk away. He bumped into Roadkill who was sporting a shit-eating grin. Angie looked up and asked, "What?"

"You're the only pipe hitter I know that uses our missions like a dating app to meet hot chicks. I think we found your callsign, Romeo," Roadkill said.

Great. At least it's not Streetwalker, he thought as he hurried away to catch up to Boss and Reaper.

***

Jon was gaining on Devilin when he saw him break into the open next to the frozen creek. Without breaking stride he stepped off the near-vertical cliff and disappeared. Lord, please, break his neck, Jon prayed. Ten seconds later, Jon stopped at the edge of the precipice and scanned the deep snow and trees fifty feet below through his GPNVGs. He saw the path Devilin had taken as he tumbled down the snow-covered rock face before he stood up at the bottom and vanished into the trees. "Well, fffffudge," Jon said, not wanting to irritate the Almighty before he jumped over the side. He was halfway to the bottom when he impacted the snow-covered rock face. The air left his lungs as he tumbled toward the bottom. Thankfully, the rock wall wasn't jagged, just hard. His body punched through the pristine snow before coming to a stop face down at the bottom of a ten-foot-deep hole. He stood up and dusted off the snow. He looked up as large clumps of snow from the rock wall continued to fall into the hole above his head. He tried to catch his breath as he assessed his situation. If he didn't start climbing out of his hole soon, he might never climb out. He brought his hands up and started trying to swim his way to the surface of the snow, but he wasn't making any progress. He was on the verge of panic when someone grabbed his arm, yanked him out of the hole, and dropped him on his back to catch his breath.

"C'mon, Jon. On your feet. Time to go get him," Michael said in encouragement.

Jon rolled over on all fours before raising himself up on his knees, "Where have you been? I told Angie about you. He thinks I'm crazy," Jon said.

"Really? I saved your life again, for what? the fourth time tonight and all you can do is whine like a two-year-old. Do you think you're my sole responsibility? Have you ever heard of multi-tasking?" Michael teased him. "Get up and go get him. He's about to take a young woman hostage."

"Dammit!" Jon shouted, as he rose to his feet and rushed off toward the trees. "Are you coming?" he asked over his shoulder. There was no response. Jon turned just in time to see Michael flying away into the blizzard on a winged red horse. *I guess minions don't get flying horses,* he thought. Jon rushed along following Devilin's trail but not actually on his trail. He didn't want to step on a landmine like Spooge had. He double-timed it through the forest as the blizzard intensified all around him. Thunder rumbled above him as lightning arced from cloud to cloud and the wind became stronger.

***

The Great Deceiver sat on his haunches atop Kintla Peak, summoning thunder and lightning over the frozen valley below him. He had assumed the form of a winged dragon, one of his favorites. He took flight, orbiting above the valley churning the blizzard to ever-increasing strength. From the opposite direction, Michael appeared on his horse flying toward the dragon at high speed. The dragon tried to stop in midair as he spewed fire at Michael. Michael flew through the flames and collided with the dragon as he stabbed at him with his lance. The dragon shrieked and flew away, pursued by Michael. Michael threw an iron chain around the dragon's neck and dragged him screaming back to Kintla Peak. Michael muzzled the dragon, pinned his wings down, and chained his legs together.

"Now, infernal beast, we will watch good destroy evil without your interference," Michael said as he dismounted and stood next to the dragon.

***

Devilin stumbled into Upper Kintla Campground 300 meters south of the Canadian border. He was lost and physically drained. It was as if a performance-enhancing drug had worn off and now he was a mere mortal again. Help was waiting for him on the Canadian side of the border. So close but out of reach. Through his NVGs, he saw several tents set up in the campground. He shouted, "Help! Is anyone here?" A light came on inside the nearest tent. "Help me!" he cried out again.

A young half-dressed couple climbed out of their small tent. "Who's there?" the young man asked as he held up a battery-powered lantern in front of them as the snow swirled around them.

"I just walked down from the glacier. I need help. Do you have a snowmobile?" Devilin asked. He saw the warm tent behind them. He wanted to kill them and borrow their tent until he recovered but he was certain more men were coming after him. *I should have hired better mercenaries*, he thought.

"No, I'm sorry. Snowmobiles are outlawed in the park, but we have several empty tents if you want to warm up and rest until the blizzard subsides," the young man replied.

"That's too bad. I guess you won't be of any help," he said before bringing forth his MP5 from behind his back and shooting the man in the chest. The man collapsed backward immediately. The young woman screamed and dropped to her knees next to him. Devilin grabbed the woman by her hair and said, "Come my dear. Let's get better acquainted."

Out of the darkness a calm, steady voice said, "Don't move Devilin. Let the girl go and I won't kill you."

Devilin spun around using the woman as a shield. He scanned the area through his NVGs but had difficulty seeing the man through the blowing snow. "I have a better idea. Throw your weapons over here or I'll kill her," he said.

"If you hurt her, I'll still kill you, but it will be a long, painful death," the man said.

"Who are you?" Devilin asked as he scanned the area for other threats.

"US Marshals Service," he replied.

"No," Devilin replied slowly, "You're one of those soldiers average Americans don't know..." He was distracted by a narrow green beam of light that dazzled his right eye before he saw a flash. The bullet destroyed his eye before scattering his brain across the snow. The woman screamed and collapsed to her knees crying. Jon rushed forward to disarm the bloody one-eyed corpse.

He turned to the woman, "Are you hit?" he asked as he checked her for wounds. She continued to wail. He grabbed her upper arms and said, "It's okay. I'm a deputy marshal. I won't let anyone hurt you," Jon said, "I'm going to check on your friend." Jon went to his knees and shined his light on the man and checked him for wounds. "Hey, he's alive. The bullet hit his collarbone and exited from his shoulder blade," Jon explained. As Jon finished applying a pressure bandage to the man, he heard the familiar roar of a Black Hawk fly past Kintla Peak. He looked up and saw the snow had lessened considerably. He could see stars in the night sky through a large break in the clouds above him. Seconds later he saw the Black Hawk descending through the opening. He switched on the IR strobe stuck to his helmet and retrieved an IR chemlight from his cargo pocket attached to a short piece of paracord. He cracked the chemlight and shook it before spinning it in a circle so the helo crew in Ghost 11 would see it.

Minutes later the helo landed next to them. Boss, Angie, and Reaper poured out and rushed toward Jon with their guns up.

"Is that Devilin?" Boss shouted in Jon's ear over the helo noise.

Jon shook his head and shouted back, "Yeah, Boss, that's him!"

"Well done, Jon!" Boss yelled as he patted him on the back. Boss leaned over the body and snapped several photos for evidence purposes. *Spooge will be glad to see this,* he thought. The helo would be crowded on the way back, so he decided to leave the body behind. The living had to go before the dead. Maybe the wolves would want him.

Angie approached Jon and shouted, "It's good to see you in one piece, mate!" as he lifted Jon off the snow with a bear hug.

"It's good to see you, too, brother!" Jon replied as Angie released him.

CHAPTER 11

1300, DECEMBER 25, DAY 2, SARAH'S PARENT'S HOME, DENVER, COLORADO

Jon saw the mistletoe hanging above the front door and smiled. He stepped forward and rang the doorbell. Seconds later, he heard footsteps rushing toward the door. Sarah threw the door open and flew into his arms. "Merry Christmas, Babe," Jon said in her ear as he lifted her off the ground.

"I was scared to death when you didn't call last night," Sarah said.

"Yeah, I'm sorry about that. My phone got wet," Jon replied. It was an enormous understatement. Jon let her down.

She took his hand and led him back inside the house. "Come up to my room and tell me everything," she said as she headed for the stairs.

"Where are your parents? Shouldn't we tell them I'm here?" he asked. He was over forty, but it felt taboo to be alone in Sarah's room without her parents' approval, especially, in their house.

"They're in the basement looking for her favorite Christmas centerpiece for the table," she said as she continued up the stairs.

Jon stopped, forcing Sarah to stop. He said, "We should tell them."

She smiled at him and said, "You're sweet." Then she turned and yelled over the railing, "Jon's here! We're going to talk in my room for a few minutes!"

"Okay, dear!" her mother shouted back from the basement.

***

Sarah's father turned to his wife and pulled her close. He smiled and said, "Since they're going to be in her room talking for a while," he emphasized the word, talking, with air quotes, "Why don't we stay down here and talk for a while?" he asked as he slowly nudged her toward their old sofa.

She kissed him and said, "You'll get your present tonight after dinner."

***

70

Sarah led Jon into her room, and they sat down on the foot of her bed. "Okay, tell me everything from the beginning."

Jon told her the whole story beginning with the canceled training exercise at the missile facility. He told her about free fall jumping onto the glacier, falling into the crevasse, and holding his breath under the ice for four minutes. Then he told her about Michael the Archangel saving his life and knowing all about him and telling him about God's love for him and his approval of what he did in Donetsk. Jon told her the guilt he had carried for years had been lifted and the tremors and eye twitches had stopped. He told her he saw Michael fight the devil and throw him into the side of a mountain. He told her about the mastodons and saving Angie, and Michael pulling him out of the deep snow before it buried him, and finally about shooting Devilin in the face before he could start his mad scientist bullshit justification speech about doing what he did for the betterment of all mankind.

"Hon, you know I love you, but can it possibly be real? Maybe you were hallucinating. Could that be possible?" she asked.

"That's what I thought when I was sitting there naked in Mike's sleeping bag. He asked me if I really believed in God, not just on Christmas and Easter, but really believed. He knew about all the times I prayed for help. I told him yes, I do believe. I couldn't have saved myself after being in the creek for so long. I never held my breath that long when I was in the teams. I couldn't have crawled out of the creek and built a snow shelter and started a fire." Jon reached into his pocket and pulled out a three-inch diameter gold coin. "I found this in my pocket," he said as he handed it to her.

The coin was worn around the edges like the owner had carried it for two thousand years. The face depicted Saint Michael riding toward her on a winged horse with his sword held above his head. It was heavy and shined bright like solid gold. She shrugged, "It's a Saint Michael's coin. So what? I have several of them."

"Flip it over," Jon replied.

She read the inscription aloud, "'Jon, God loves you. Continue your mission to protect his children, Michael.' Oh, my Lord!" Sarah said as she covered her mouth.

THE END

Thank you for reading CHRISTMAS REDEMPTION. I sincerely hope you enjoyed it. Please, do me a huge favor and leave a review on Amazon. Indie authors, like me, struggle to get reviews for our books. I've read typically only one of 200 readers leave a review. Reviews on Amazon help move my book up in the rankings and give me a more competitive chance as I compete with more well established authors.

Also, please join my newsletter using the link below for updates on future Jon Smith novels and short stories and I will give you a FREE copy of my Jon Smith Short Story, SMOKE SIGNALS. I promise I won't sell or share your email address with others.

Bob Asher Books Newsletter

NOW, PLEASE ENJOY

A SNEAK PEEK OF MY

NEXT JON SMITH NOVEL

BOOK #3

FLASH OVERRIDE

CHAPTER 1

Jon and Angie sat next to each other in the cargo area of the L-100 cargo plane eating piping hot Zurek soup in sourdough bread bowls. They hadn't expected to eat during the flight but since they were the only passengers, their Polish flight crew shared their in-flight meal with them. They wolfed down the hearty soup and the bread bowl.

"Man, that was good. I don't know what was in it but it really hit the spot," Jon said appreciatively. He licked his MRE spoon clean and stuffed it back in his pocket. Professional soldiers always had a spoon close by just in case they came across an opportunity to eat something. The smart ones also carried a miniature bottle of Tabasco sauce.

"Yeah, it was great. It reminds me of my Ukrainian grandmother's soup. I think it's called Zurek. She made something similar when I was a kid. It was full of kielbasa, ham, boiled eggs, potatoes, and onions but this one was a lot spicier than hers," Angie replied. Angie was Jon's battle buddy, retired Warrant Officer Angus Hawkins of the Australian Special Air Service Regiment. They were in the insertion phase of their mission, a mission that started four months earlier in Ukraine when they rescued a nun and 91 Ukrainian orphans from corrupt Chechen soldiers. The soldiers were human traffickers who were selling the children to the highest bidder to be used in the sex trade or to be murdered for their vital organs. They paid for their transgressions with their lives. Jon and Angie's final target, the broker who arranged the sales of thousands of children, eluded them. In the coming days, they would finish what they started.

***

An hour later, the loadmaster's hands alternated between the bulkhead and cargo nets as he shuffled his way down the narrow path between the cargo pallets and the red nylon troop seats to talk to his only passengers. They were strapped into seats near the ramp of the white and blue Lockheed L-100 also known as a Hercules. It was a civilian version of the military C-130 tactical cargo plane. CIA Paramilitary Operations Officer Jon Smith sat with his boots crossed on top of his pack and a paperback in his hands. He had his blue LED headlamp turned on so he could read Alice York's latest Amish romance/action thriller titled Black Hawk Down on the Farm as the aircraft shook and shimmied its way across the foreboding sky. Angie was lying beside him in his sleeping bag, peacefully snoring the night away.

The loadmaster tapped Jon's boot to get his attention. He motioned to Angie. Jon removed one of his foam earplugs and shook Angie's shoulder. "We are on approach to Chisinau International but the ceiling and visibility are down to 700 feet and a mile and there's sleet and freezing rain in the vicinity. How badly do you need to get in there tonight?" the loadmaster asked in thickly accented English loud enough to be heard over the four Allison turboprop engines. Each was putting out 4,510 shaft horsepower.

"Not bad enough to spend my final minutes screaming in terror before I burn alive. How about you Angie?" Jon asked.

Angie looked up to the loadmaster and replied, "No thanks. I'm good with living to fight another day, and ah, thanks for the soup, mate. It was delicious." Jon nodded his agreement. Angie put his head back down in the bag.

The loadmaster smiled and threw them a thumbs up before turning to walk back the way he came.

Jon stretched and twisted his back and neck as he sat on the uncomfortable nylon bench seat. As he scanned the cabin's ceiling he noticed four olive drab parachutes hanging from the rafters. "Hey Angie, look at this," he said as he pointed to the parachutes. "That seems awfully optimistic, don't you think?"

Angie peeked out of his bag and asked, "What do you mean?"

"Well, there are four guys on the aircrew and four parachutes hanging up there. If the plane starts going down what makes them think we're going to just sit here and let them put those parachutes on?" Jon asked.

"They might get away with it if they don't wake me up," Angie replied before his head disappeared again.

Within a couple of minutes, the shaking and shimming became severe. The plane dropped abruptly like a broken elevator. If Jon and Angie weren't belted down they would have smacked into the overhead.

Suddenly, Angie wasn't sleepy anymore. His head popped out of the bag and he said, "What the hell was that, mate?"

"I don't know," Jon said as he shined his light around the cargo area and pallets in front of them.

The loadmaster hurried down the path to them again. He yelled, "Ice is building up on the wings and fuselage. We're committed to landing at Chisinau now. Stay strapped in and you'll be fine. You're in the safest seats on the airplane!" He gave them another thumbs up and rushed away toward the cockpit.

"That's funny, I don't feel safer!" Jon shouted to Angie who was now sitting up, out of his sleeping bag, with his OD green Ops-Core Fast SF High Cut helmet on.

"Why can't we fly commercial like civilized people?" Angie complained. The L-100 bucked violently.

"When have you ever been accused of being civilized?" Jon replied. He looked around, "Are we flying sideways?" His inner ear was telling him the left wing had dropped and he felt weight build up on his back as he was pressed against his nylon web seatback. Jon's eyes went wide as a heavy-duty tie-down strap holding the cargo pallet in place popped loose between his feet and flapped back and forth several feet from his face. The pallet shifted ever so slightly toward him, causing him to reflexively pull his feet back. Jon reached for the strap but his seat belt held him back. He released his seat belt just in time for the plane to return to level flight momentarily before the right wing dropped. He was thrown into the side of the pile of cargo before falling up to the ceiling and then onto the floor on the other side of the pallet. Stars danced before his eyes. The plane slowly returned to wings level.

"Are you all right, Jonny?" Angie shouted. He couldn't see Jon over the top of the cargo.

"No!" Jon replied annoyed. He blinked hard to clear the stars as he started climbing over the cargo using the cargo net for handholds. He clambered over the top and dropped down on the left side where he tried to get the cargo strap back in place. He pulled on the strap with all his strength until his arms quivered but he was still two inches short. "Angie, help me!" he yelled over the engines. Angie dropped to his knees and held the pad eye ring up. Jon quickly hooked the strap to it before ratcheting it tight. They didn't waste any time getting their seat belts back on. Then they sat anxiously waiting for the plane to disintegrate around them.

The noise level inside the cargo area lessened as the pilot throttled back on the engines to decelerate and lowered the nose to descend. Sounds they had heard hundreds of times before during their careers now sounded foreign and frightening. "What is that? Is something wrong with the engines?" Angie asked. He and Jon shared concerned looks.

"Shit! I don't know!" Jon replied. "Angie, why don't you climb up there and get a couple of those parachutes for us?" Jon asked.

"Fuck you, mate!" Angie replied.

Next, they heard electric motors activating to lower the flaps on the wings to increase the lift they provided. "Fuck! It sounds like something is scraping against the wings," Jon said.

Other motors lowered the landing gear. Jon felt a thump from behind as the left main mount locked into place. "The plane's coming apart!" He felt sick to his stomach. He grabbed an air sickness bag from the holder attached to the bulkhead behind him and spewed the yummy soup into it. Angie, being a sympathetic puker, was five seconds behind him. They had been sitting there for five minutes praying for salvation while holding their partially digested bags of Zurek when the wheels contacted the pavement of Runway 08.

The pilot reversed the pitch on the propellers to rapidly slow the plane before he turned off on the midfield taxiway and headed for the parking ramp. A follow-me truck met them and led them to their parking spot. As they came to a stop Jon saw the loadmaster climbing down the steps from the cockpit. Jon quickly said, "Take this!" and handed off his puke bag to Angie.

"Hey, hold on, mate!" Angie complained as he held the bag gingerly at arm's length like it contained Ebola.

Jon swiftly opened his pack and pulled out a two-gallon Ziplock bag with a clean change of clothes in it. He removed the clothes and stuffed them back into the pack. Jon grabbed both airsickness bags, secured them inside the Ziplock bag, and put it back in his pack right before the loadmaster stepped over their legs to get to the rear of the plane. Jon turned to Angie and said, "This never happened. If the team got wind of it they'd memorialize it somehow on the wall of shame in the team room right next to the photo you took of my naked ass in the Suburban." He was referring to an incident in Ukraine four months earlier when they came under attack while Angie was driving down the highway as Jon stood in the backseat trying to take a shit in another two-gallon Ziplock bag. The bags were extremely versatile and a favorite in the special operations community. Russian separatists in two technicals opened fire on them and Jon stood up in the open sunroof to return fire with his trousers down around his ankles. Angie took a smiling selfie with Jon's bare ass beyond Angie's right shoulder so he could share the moment with the entire fucking intelligence community.

Angie smiled and said, "What never happened?"

The loadmaster lowered the ramp and they shouldered their packs before walking down the ramp onto the pavement. The concrete was slick with a thin layer of ice. A light but steady curtain of sleet was falling as a silver Toyota Land Cruiser pulled up next to the ramp and a short man wearing a green camouflaged Gortex jacket hopped out from the front passenger side. "Jon, it's good to see you, my friend. Welcome back to Chisinau," he said with a smile.

"It's good to see you too, Cujo," Jon said as they hugged. "This is my friend, Angus Hawkins."

"It is good to meet you, Angus. I am Major Maximilian Cojocari, but please, call me Cujo," he said as they shook hands.

"Good to meet you, too, mate. You can call me Angie," he replied.

"Come. Let us get out of this miserable weather," Cujo said as they hurried to the car. Cujo's driver, his oldest son, quickly maneuvered them off the airport and onto the highway. Cujo's head was on a swivel. He had made many enemies during his twenty-five-year intel career. He alternated his attention between the highway and his guests. Cujo leaned over his seat back to talk to Jon and Angie. "The weather is too bad for you to continue your flight tonight. You will stay at my house and continue tomorrow night when the weather will be good."

"Are you sure? What about Maria?" Jon asked. Maria was Cujo's wife.

"Maria loves you. I called her. She is happy you are coming. She has a late dinner prepared. It's very good. She made a Polish soup called Zurek," Cujo reassured him.

"Great, that sounds terrific," Jon said to the back of Cujo's head as he exchanged an uneasy look with Angie.

Cujo fished some papers out of his pocket. "Have you seen these?" Cujo asked as he handed two wanted posters to Jon.

Jon studied Angie's poster and laughed at the sketch of his face. He looked like a rather mannish Catholic nun wearing Ray-ban Wayfarer sunglasses. He handed it to Angie, who cringed. "Certainly not my finest hour."

Jon looked at his own wanted poster. "This is bullshit, this looks nothing like me!" Jon complained.

Angie snatched it from his hand. "I don't know, mate. It looks accurate to me. Perhaps the eyes could be a bit beadier," he said.

"Sure, it does, in a menacing serial killer sort of way," Jon replied.

"Well, you did look quite menacing when you were driving your knife down into Sultanovich's neck and you racked up a rather spectacular body count that day. Hey, look at this," Angie said with pride as he pointed at the posters, "I'm worth twice as much as you."

"What? Let me see that!" Jon grabbed the posters. His eyes went back and forth between them. "Son of a bitch!" Angie was worth one hundred million Russian rubles which converted to a little over $1,000,000. Jon's was only fifty million.

"Maybe you need a better press agent," Angie teased.

CHAPTER 2

1200 LOCAL, THURSDAY, JANUARY 30, DAY 1, HIGHWAY D FARMHOUSE, ST. FRANCOIS COUNTY

A red, white, and blue cement truck from A2Z Concrete drove up the gravel driveway and stopped in front of the house. The driver sent out two quick blasts from his air horn. A man stepped out from behind the house and waved the driver forward. He guided him to stop next to a 15×30 foot hole in the ground. Concrete steps ended ten feet below the ground above. What looked like a concrete foundation with a nine-foot pour was covered with a heavy-duty corrugated metal roof and a rebar matrix to reinforce it. The driver climbed out of the cab and was met by a dark-skinned man who spoke with an odd accent. "Good morning, sir. I'm Floyd Greene. What can I do for you?" he asked.

"Good morning, sir. I need a six-inch thick roof poured on top of this foundation," the man said in English. It was obvious to

Greene that the man was a highly educated foreigner from one of those countries whose names ended in stan. Four other men stood by waiting with tools and rubber boots.

"That's a lot of concrete. Are you sure the roof can support it?" Greene asked.

The man seemed perturbed. "Yes, I am quite certain. I am a civil engineer. I have done the calculations. It is more than strong enough. Please, begin the pour," he said.

Greene nodded. "Okay, sir, you got it," he said. *It'll be fun watching that roof crumple up like an empty beer can,* he thought. He started pouring and said, "Just say when."

After the proper amount of concrete was received the engineer signaled for Greene to stop and joined the others to finish the concrete roof. Greene hosed the chute clean and retrieved the clipboard that held the invoice from the cab. He set it on the rear fender while he waited for the roof to collapse, but it held. While the men worked, he decided to go down the steps and take a look inside the bunker, storm shelter, or root cellar, whatever it was. He walked down the wide stairs and stopped at a heavy gray steel commercial door. He turned the knob and pushed it open. The room was dark except for what little light made it down the stairs. He stuck his head inside and waved his cell phone light around. He found a light switch on the wall next to the door and flipped it on. Overhead fluorescent lights bathed the large room in bright blue tinted light. It was empty except for five large steel eyebolts embedded waist-high in the far wall. Sex dungeon. Kinky, he thought as he flipped the lights off and walked back up the stairs. He was met by the engineer who handed him the clipboard. He had already signed it. Greene peeled off his copy and gave it to him. "Here you go, sir. Let us know if you need anything else," he said. He turned to look at the roof. "The roof looks great. You guys do good work." He climbed into the truck and drove away.

A silver Mercedes sedan passed the cement truck on the gravel driveway going in the opposite direction. The man wearing a dark gray suit parked behind the house and walked over to the bunker. "Excellent work, brothers. Soon we will be done with this God-forsaken country and we can go home," he said in Chechen. The men gathered around him.

"We may have a problem, Mukhamed," the engineer said to his brother.

"What is it, Khamza? The roof looks fine," Mukhamed asked.

"While we were distracted finishing the roof, the driver went down the stairs and looked inside. I am certain he saw the eye-bolts," Khamza said.

"I see. I realize Father put me in charge because I am the oldest but I have no experience in these matters. I will continue to rely on all of your expertise. Should we silence this man?" he asked the group.

The fourth son, a soldier, Alvi spoke up. "We cannot risk leaving him alive. He could ruin the plan before we get started. Solta, Dokka, and I will take care of it tonight. We will make it look like an accident or suicide." The others nodded their agreement.

CHAPTER 3

"I'm already hating this," Jon transmitted on his team radio from underneath his oxygen mask, "It's going to be minus 40°F outside when we jump." He liked jumping out of airplanes almost as much as he enjoyed long underwater ocean swims, which was not at all. There was so much that could go wrong. You could do everything right and still die horribly. He and Angie were pre-breathing 100% oxygen for 45 minutes before they jumped off the ramp of the L-100 from flight level 230 which was 7,000 meters or 23,000 ft. They were wearing insulated jumpsuits over their civilian clothes to ward off the bitter cold.

"No worries, mate. It'll all be over in a few minutes. Ground temp is a balmy 30°F," Angie teased.

"I better not break my leg before I get to kill this motherfucker," Jon whined.

"Remind me again why you became a SEAL?" Angie asked. Jon's answer was always different.

"My recruiter told me I could fly Hornets but he signed me up as a culinary specialist. No way was I going to clean tables and wash dishes for six years. My only options to get out of it in boot camp were volunteering for SEAL or EOD training. Those crazy EOD fucks jump and swim like SEALS except they get the added fun of defusing 2,000-pound bombs. Screw that," Jon replied.

"Would you prefer something smaller, say a misfired 40mm grenade?" Angie asked.

"Fuck no, I don't want to go blind or lose my hands. I would rather it be one of those big mothers. That way here one second, gone the next," Jon replied.

Angie laughed. "If you don't like jumping why do you keep doing it?" he asked.

Jon shrugged, "I guess I just like being around the type of people who like to jump. You know, crazy fuckers, like you," Jon replied.

Angie laughed as the loadmaster walked past them. He motioned for them to stand up. He held up his thumb and two fingers.

Jon checked Angie's parachute and gear. He slapped him on the shoulder and said, "You're good." Jon turned around so Angie could check his.

Angie ran his hands over Jon's parachute and tactical gear and said, "I don't know Jonny; I don't think I'd jump with this parachute," Angie feigned concern.

"Ha-ha, fuck you, dickhead," Jon said as he held up his middle finger while waddling toward the ramp. Angie followed close behind. The loadmaster lowered the ramp to the level position. "Damn, that's cold!" Jon complained as the burble of frigid air came inside the cargo compartment. He lowered his NVGs over his clear-lensed Wiley goggles and stepped onto the ramp. The loadmaster wearing a helmet and oxygen mask of his own pointed at Jon and then turned, knelt down on one knee, and pointed off the ramp like he was a shooter or Navy catapult officer launching a Hornet off an aircraft carrier. Everyone's a comedian, Jon thought. He walked to the edge of the ramp and dove head-first into the dark abyss. Angie was two seconds behind him. They planned to free fall to 3,000 feet before popping their chutes.

"Gabby, please, tell me you're down there," Jon transmitted on the team radio as he reached terminal velocity, approximately 126 MPH.

"Roger that, I see you. I'm standing by," she replied.

"Is the van warmed up?" Jon asked.

"Affirm. I even brought some hot chocolate and cookies," Gabby said.

"You know, you've always been my favorite," Jon said as he scanned the area for threats with his GPNVGs. The countryside was dark except for an occasional farmhouse. "Give us a vector."

"Steer 090° for three miles. When you get close I'll flip on my IR strobe," Gabby replied.

CHAPTER 4

The three brothers walked quietly across the field that backed up to Greene's house. He owned a two-acre lot on Highway K that was surrounded on three sides by cow pastures. The fence row was overgrown with bushes and weeds. They stopped at the fence, watched, and listened in the darkness. The fence did not continue around to the front of the house. "When Solta and I followed Greene home yesterday afternoon we did not see anyone else. We think he lives alone. The nearest house is 500 meters to the south," Alvi said.

"Does he have any dogs?" Dokka asked.

"None outside. I do not know about inside his house. Our boots are muddy. We must take them off before we go inside. Pull your masks down and keep your gloves on. He may have hidden cameras," Alvi said.

They covered their faces with ski masks and scaled the welded wire fence. They walked silently across the backyard and tried the sliding door. It opened. They sat on the edge of the small concrete patio and removed their boots. They opened the door again and Alvi turned on a dim blue LED light to help them see. They walked across the finished basement and checked the bedroom and adjacent bathroom. They were empty. Alvi led the way up the stairs. Upon opening the door on the first floor, he could hear Greene snoring on the second floor. "Clear this floor. I will go upstairs to watch Greene," Alvi whispered to his brothers. Moments later, Alvi stood in the open doorway to Greene's bedroom watching him snore. The room reeked of stale beer. He was soon joined by Solta and Dokka. Alvi readied the syringe of Propofol his older brother, the doctor provided. Mukhamed assured them it would render Greene unconscious in seconds. Solta and Dokka each held down one of Greene's arms as Alvi injected the Propofol into his neck.

"Hey, what the fuck is going on? Help! Help me!" Greene shouted into the darkness as he struggled before quickly falling silent. After a minute Solta and Dokka released their death grips on Greene's arms.

"Dokka, stay with him. Solta and I will have a look around to see what we can use for his suicide," Alvi said.

Dokka picked up Greene's cell phone off the bedside table and held it up to Greene's face to unlock it. He read through his most recent messages.

Alvi and Solta came back a few minutes later.

Dokka held up the phone. "His girlfriend broke up with him a week ago. He has been begging her to come back to him but she ignored his calls and texts. Last night he was suspended from his job for failing a drug test," Dokka said.

"Good that gives him reasons to hurt himself. There is an SKS rifle in the closet. We can use it to kill him. People in America like to kill themselves in bathtubs. It's easier to clean up. There is a bathtub in the basement. Let's take him down there. Is there a bucket in the house?" Alvi asked.

"Yes, there are several in the garage," Solta replied.

"Dokka, When we are ready. Text her that he will kill himself if she does not come to him right away. Then you and Solta watch from outside and let me know when she gets here. I'll shoot him when she gets inside so she can report hearing him shoot himself," Alvi said.

A half hour later the messages had been sent and the brothers were waiting in position. Headlights appeared a couple of miles down the highway. The car sped toward the house and slowed abruptly to pull into the driveway. "A car just arrived and a woman is running toward the front door," Solta said over his cell phone from his hidden vantage point behind the thick bushes in the fence row.

"Perhaps it would be better if this were a murder-suicide," Alvi proposed from the basement. The body was staged in the bathtub.

"Wait! A police car is coming with its emergency lights on. She must have called them before she drove here," Solta replied.

"All right, I will wait until the police are inside so they can hear the gunshot," Alvi said. He heard the woman open the unlocked front door and run upstairs to look for Floyd. Seconds later she came back to the first floor. Floyd wasn't there either. She tried the basement door and found it locked. She cried out for Floyd to unlock the door. Next Alvi heard the police knock on the front door.

CHAPTER 5

0525 FRIDAY, FRIDAY, JANUARY 31, DAY 2, ST. FRANCOIS COUNTY SHERIFF'S DEPARTMENT STATION

"Welcome back, Brother. How was Alabama?" Deputy Kurt Sada asked his temporary partner and trainee as they sat in the front row of tables in the St. Francois County, Missouri Sheriff's Department squad room waiting for shift change to start.

"It sucked being away from home for two months, but it wasn't all bad. The weather was warmer than it is up here and learning to fly the Black Hawk was a blast. After a couple of weeks, Patty flew down to Pensacola and we spent the weekend together. Then Patty and Danny came down to Rucker to see me over the Thanksgiving break. The extra money was nice," Deputy Zack Goodson replied. Zack had recently transferred his reserve commission from the Marine Corps to the Missouri Army National Guard and accepted orders to Fort Novosel, Alabama to go through transition training on the UH-60 Black Hawk helicopter. The Army called it the Aircraft Qualification Course. Now that he was a qualified copilot he would be working full-time as a deputy sheriff and part-time as a soldier.

"Mind if I ask how much they pay?"

"As a captain with eleven years of service with flight pay, it was a little over twenty grand before taxes for two months."

"Shit! That's six months' pay for me. I need to talk to your recruiter."

"The money's pretty good for officers, but if you sign up, you'll earn every penny. Did I miss anything interesting while I was gone?"

"A couple of weeks ago Daryl Ballard from Leadwood PD almost shot his dick off?"

"No shit! How'd he do that?"

"He was off duty having lunch at the Catfish Kettle with a friend of his. Daryl was telling him about his new Diamondback DB9 pistol. Have you ever seen one?"

Zack shook his head.

"It's a little polymer 9mm pocket gun and great for a backup because you can stick it in a pocket holster in your back pocket and it looks like a wallet. So, after they got done eating, they both went out to Daryl's truck so he could show him the pistol. They climbed in the cab and Daryl pulled the pistol out of his pocket still in the little nylon holster. He unloaded it and handed it to his buddy. He admired it for a minute and handed it back to Daryl. Daryl reloaded it and went to put it back in the holster. He was holding the holster between his legs with his left hand and began putting the pistol in the holster with his right hand when he realized his finger was in the trigger guard. He said his mind was screaming at his hand to stop, but it kept moving toward the holster. When his finger hit the edge of the holster the pistol fired and put a round through the inside of his left thigh a couple of inches from his junk. The bullet was an FMJ, so it went through the seat and stuck in the floor. People in the parking lot heard the shot and called 911. Then Daryl's buddy called 911 for an ambulance and told them Officer Ballard was shot in the leg. Dispatch put out an officer had been shot, so within five minutes ten police cars rolled into the parking lot.

"Damn, is he all right?"

"He's still on light duty walking around their station bow-legged, but yeah, he'll be okay. He does have a new nickname."

"What's that?" Zack smiled.

"Do you remember when Walter Brennan played the limping deputy in Rio Bravo?"

"Stumpy?"

"Yep, that's it." They both laughed.

The morning Watch Commander, Lieutenant Ike McLeod, entered the squad room and walked over to Kurt and Zack. "We already have a call. It's an attempted suicide." He handed Kurt a piece of paper with the address on it. "Get over there and see what's happening. Let me know if you need more help. Welcome back, Zack," he smiled.

***

"Central, ten-oh-five, 10-23," Zack transmitted over the cruiser's radio. 10-23 meant they had arrived at the farmhouse on Highway D.

"Ten-oh-five, 10-23, at 0549," Peggy, the Central County 911 dispatcher replied.

It was still dark as they approached the house cautiously with their Glocks held down along the sides of their legs. As they reached the porch, the front door flew open and a woman hurried outside. They could see by the porch light she had tears on her face. Before they could speak, she said, "Please, help me! He's going to kill himself!"

"Ma'am, who is he and is he armed?" Kurt asked.

"My boyfriend, Floyd locked himself in the basement. He's going to…" A gunshot thundered from inside the home. The woman screamed and yelled, "No!"

Zack and Kurt pushed past the woman with their guns aimed down the hall. Zack saw a stairway leading to the second floor. He went further down the hall and grabbed the knob on the basement door.

"The door's locked from the other side and it opens outward," Zack said. He pounded on the door with the bottom of his fist. "The door's hollow." He stepped back and kicked it. His boot went through the door and Kurt caught him before he could fall. Zack pulled his leg out of the hole and reached inside to unlock the knob. He opened the door.

Kurt stepped in front. "I'll go first." The lights were on in the basement. He called out, "Floyd, are you okay? We're here to help you! Call out if you hear me!"

Floyd's girlfriend was behind them. "Help him! He could be dying!"

"Ma'am, we're trying. Go wait by the front door. Zack, call for backup and an ambulance."

Zack made the call on his walkie.

"You have to help him. Don't just stand there." She tried to push past them. They stopped her.

"Go cuff her to the upstairs railing," Kurt said.

She refused to move so Zack picked her up around her waist and carried her back down the hall toward the front door. He handcuffed her left wrist to the cast iron railing leading upstairs and rejoined Kurt. They carefully moved down the stairs into the basement. Half of it was finished as a man cave.

"Floyd, where are you? Are you okay?" Kurt called out. There was no response. "Let's clear this room and then we'll check that bedroom back there." Kurt cleared the right side of the large room and Zack cleared the left side which included a homemade bar. They met at the bedroom doorway. They could smell blood and acrid gun smoke in the air. Kurt entered first. He could see across the room into the bathroom. "He's in the bathtub. I think he's dead." Kurt entered the bathroom with his Glock pointed at the body. He paused for a moment and holstered his pistol. "We're clear."

Zack entered behind him and they stood next to each other looking at the body. The man was wearing a gray "I Support the Right to Arm Bears" T-shirt and plaid boxers. A galvanized steel bucket was pulled down over his head. A cheap Chinese SKS rifle rested against his chest. It appeared he had stuck the barrel under his chin and pulled the trigger. The 7.62mm bullet had passed through his head and punched a hole in the bottom of the bucket. It broke one of the ceramic tiles in the wall behind him, but then the bullet ran out of energy and fell back into the tub between his legs. The bloody mess was contained within the bucket and to the top of his shirt. "I wonder why he did it. It looks like he had a nice place here," Zack wondered out loud.

"I don't know. Let's go ask her." Kurt said as he put on a pair of black nitrile gloves. They walked back upstairs.

As soon as they came into view, she asked, "Is he all right?"

"No, I'm sorry, he's not. It appears he shot himself. He's dead," Kurt replied.

She sat down on the stairs and cried.

"Zack, call Ike, on your cell phone and tell him what happened."

Zack walked outside onto the porch. "Hey, Lieutenant. It's Zack. The guy shot himself in the head right after we got here. His girlfriend is crying uncontrollably. We need the coroner and a detective out here."

"We don't have a detective right now. Mark's still on light duty rehabbing his arm, so he can't leave the station. You guys will have to handle the investigation. I'll call Les and get him heading your way," Lieutenant McLeod replied. Mark was Detective Sergeant Mark Langford. He had been shot in the left arm during an ambush about six months earlier in June by a crazed father who went on a killing spree after his daughter was found murdered. Zack had been with him during the ambush and saved his life. Les was the elected County Coroner, Lester Koplin. He also owned Koplin Funeral Home in Park Hills.

"Okay, sir. We're on it." Zack hung up and went back inside. Kurt had removed the woman's handcuffs. She was still sitting on the steps crying. "Ike said no detective today, we're it."

Kurt handed the handcuffs to Zack and nodded. "Yeah, that's what I figured." He turned back to the woman. She was beginning to regain her composure. What's your name ma'am?" Kurt asked.

"Brandy Carson."

"Do you live here?"

"No. I live with my mother in Park Hills."

Kurt wrote her name in his notebook. "What's his name?"

"Floyd Greene," she said.

"Ma'am, can you tell us why he would want to harm himself?" Kurt asked.

"I broke up with him last week and he started calling me constantly. After a few days, I stopped answering his calls. Then he started texting me. I didn't answer the texts either. About an hour ago he texted me that he was going to kill himself," she said.

"Where did he work?" Kurt asked.

"He drove a cement truck for that place, A2Z Concrete, south of Bonne Terre off Vo-Tech Road. They laid him off last night because he failed a drug test," she said.

"What was he using?" Kurt asked.

"Meth and a little weed," she said.

"Where was he getting it?" Kurt asked.

"I don't know?" she said.

"Do you use?" Kurt asked.

"No!" she feigned offense. "Is that all? Can I go now?"

"Yes, ma'am. We'll be in touch," Kurt replied.

She got up off the stairs and stomped out the front door.

"I guess you hit a nerve," Zack said as he watched her walk down the front steps.

"She probably got the drugs for him. She already has some signs of meth abuse on her face. In a year or two she'll look fifteen years older," Kurt said. "Why don't you go take some pictures and secure his rifle and that bullet."

***

An hour and a half later, Lester Koplin arrived in his van with his assistant, Timmy. They dragged their gurney across the yard and up the stairs. "Sorry, we took so long, boys. Where is he?" Koplin asked.

"He's in the basement. Follow me," Zack said.

"How was Rucker?" Timmy asked.

Zack looked up at the giant. "They changed the name. It's Novosel now. The flying was great, but I was ready to come home." He led them down the narrow basement stairs. All four of them gathered in the small bathroom.

Koplin took a minute to put on a pair of blue nitrile gloves. He looked over the body and the bucket. "This is one of the most considerate suicide victims I've ever seen. He kept the mess contained to the tub. Did you guys already take your pictures?"

"Yeah, we're good," Zack said.

Koplin leaned over to lift the bucket off the head. They heard the vacuum releasing as he raised the bucket. The bullet hole in the bottom of the bucket made it easier. As the bucket came off, the head separated in the middle and fell over on both shoulders.

The brain matter slid down the front of his shirt. Zack turned away and puked all over the toilet.

Kurt was mesmerized by the grotesque headless body. "Man, that's fucked up! It smells as bad as it looks!" He leaned in next to Koplin and pointed to the left shoulder. "Is that an eyeball?" Zack hurled again as he held the toilet bowl. Kurt turned to see Zack convulsing and grinned. "You gonna be all right, Devil Dog?" Zack gave him a thumbs up and stuck his head in the sink to rinse his mouth out.

FLASH OVERRIDE Release Planned for Winter 2025

ABOUT THE AUTHOR

Bob is a retired supervisory intelligence officer with the National Geospatial-Intelligence Agency (NGA). He grew up in and around St. Louis, Missouri. By the time he was in high school he knew he wanted to do two things with his life: fly in the military and work in law enforcement. After graduating from Parks College of St. Louis University with a degree in Aeronautics he earned a commission in the USMC. He became a Naval Aviator flying the CH-53D Sea Stallion helicopter. After his active duty, he returned to the St. Louis area and worked as a police officer. When the Twin Towers were attacked, he joined the Missouri Army National Guard and flew

Black Hawk helicopters in Iraq during Operation Iraqi Freedom II. While in Iraq he applied for and accepted a position with NGA. Now he and his wife live a quiet life in the country surrounded by trees.

www.ingramcontent.com/pod-product-compliance
Lightning Source LLC
Chambersburg PA
CBHW052014170626
46808CB00007B/2925

* 9 7 8 1 9 5 8 1 1 5 0 6 0 *